It's Crystal Clear

Nancy had better shape up. Or so says Jeremy, the twisted teenager who lives with her and her aunt. That's no idle threat, either. Ever since he got his hands on the shape-shifter, a powerful and magical crystal, Jeremy has had the power to bend anyone and anything to his will. Now he's threatening to turn Nancy into a one-woman horror show and she's powerless to stop him. Or is she?

THE TRAP DOOR

Copyright © 1995 by RGA Publishing Group, Inc.

Published by Troll Associates, Inc. Rainbow Bridge is a trademark of Troll Associates. Screamers is a trademark of RGA Publishing Group, Inc.

Printed in the United States of America.

10 9 8 7 6 5 4 3 2 1

SCREAMERS™

THE TRAP DOOR
& Other Stories to Twist Your Mind

by Don Wulffson

Rainbow Bridge®
Troll Associates

CONTENTS

THE SHAPE-SHIFTER

"It's been going on too long now," I tell my Aunt Hattie. "It's sick and completely out of hand. I'm so nervous I've bitten all my nails off, until my fingers bleed."

"Don't talk so loud, Nancy," Aunt Hattie whispers. "Jeremy will hear you."

"Yeah, well, something's got to be done about him. I don't care if he is almost like a son to you."

My aunt knows I'm right, but she moves away from me. She doesn't want to talk about Jeremy—ever. Instead she starts dusting and polishing the antiques and handicrafts in her shop, most of which are Native American. There are beads, amulets, hunting pouches, baskets, and even an authentic war canoe hanging from wires from the ceiling.

I have nothing better to do, so I grab a feather duster and start helping out. Working helps me relax, and sort of makes my mind go blank. For a moment I almost forget about Jeremy.

Then I hear the floorboards creak up on the second floor, up in his bedroom. I see Aunt Hattie stiffen. As for me, it takes all I can do to keep from gnawing on my fingernails. We both listen as his door opens, then closes. Then we hear his footsteps coming down the stairs.

"Good morning, everyone," he says cheerily, walking into the shop.

Both of us politely return the greeting, then go back to work.

From his jacket pocket, Jeremy takes the crystal and begins turning it over and over in his hand. I begin to sweat and I see Aunt Hattie darting quick little looks in his direction.

"Don't look at me," Jeremy says to her.

"I wasn't," she responds nervously.

"Now you're lying to me!" he scolds her.

"I wasn't!" she insists.

"Bite your tongue!" he says, then breaks into an ugly fit of laughter.

Aunt Hattie starts chewing on her tongue, biting it hard over and over again. Soon little drops of blood begin dripping onto the new white dress she is wearing. I can see Aunt Hattie is in great pain, but she can't stop.

"I really wish you'd stop that," Jeremy finally says.

Aunt Hattie is holding her hand over her mouth, but I can see that she has finally stopped chewing on her tongue.

Jeremy sits down in a rustic wood-and-leather chair. He smiles at Aunt Hattie, then he turns his attention to me. It's my turn. I smile weakly back at him, hoping he'll be nice and give me a break today.

"You have a nice smile, Nancy," he says. "Smile more."

Instantly, my lips peel back from my teeth and gums, and I smile idiotically. I look like the chimpanzees at the zoo when they screech and smile with their big, crazy grins. My smile is getting so big it is stretching my face. It hurts, but I can't stop smiling no matter what I do. Only Jeremy can make me stop. Or, if he chooses, he can leave me like this for the rest of my life.

"Quit smiling," he says.

My face relaxes. It still hurts a little, and my mouth feels weird, but at least the ridiculous smile is gone.

"Get back to work," says Jeremy, "both of you."

I look at his rotten thirteen-year-old brat face smirking at us, and I'd like to wring his neck. But, like Aunt Hattie, I do what I'm told. We have to.

As we work, the two of us exchange glances. Her outfit is ruined and her tongue must hurt like crazy. Me, all I got was an insane smile stuck on my face for awhile. All in all, we've both gotten off really easy today . . . so far.

* * *

It all started when my parents decided to take a second honeymoon and tour Europe for their tenth anniversary. While they were gone, from June to August, I was left with my Aunt Hattie, which is okay, because I like her. She gives me fifty dollars a week for helping out around her shop, and I get my own room. It's right next to Jeremy's, on the second floor, upstairs from the shop.

If it hadn't have been for Jeremy, a street kid my aunt took in years ago out of the goodness of her heart, there wouldn't have been any problems at all. But ever since I've known him, Jeremy has been weird. He's always had a fascination with gross stuff, like bats, lizards, snakes, and anything dead. I remember how, when I was little, he had a medical book that showed actual corpses. The book also showed how doctors do dissections, and it had pictures of them doing organ transplants. It made me sick to look at the book. The pictures still give me nightmares. But Jeremy told me he loved looking at the book, and that he wanted to be a doctor just so he could cut people open.

So, needless to say, when I found out about my parents' second honeymoon and that I'd have to be around Jeremy all summer, I got pretty stressed out. But I thought being with my aunt and having lots of freedom would make up for it. And actually, at first Jeremy wasn't so bad. It wasn't until Desmond Newflower, a little old Native American man, came into Aunt Hattie's shop that everything turned into a living nightmare.

Mr. Newflower came in under the pretense of wanting to sell us stuff like handwoven blankets and wall hangings, but he actually had something else in mind entirely. I remember the guy was real tense, and he seemed less concerned about making a sale than about getting rid of this odd pink crystal. His hands trembled when he opened the little cedar box he kept it in, and he made a big deal about it when he showed it to us. My aunt thought it was pretty, and possibly of some value, so she asked Mr. Newflower to tell us about it. He eagerly launched right into a story.

"Long ago, the crystal was unearthed with some very old graves that were found on a reservation where my tribe once lived," he said. "Since then, it has become part of my heritage. We call it a shape-shifter." His eyes sparkled when he said the word. "Its owner can get whatever he or she wants when holding the crystal, but I am not comfortable with its power." He held the odd gem out toward my aunt. "May I give it to you?" he asked nervously.

It seemed to me that the old man wanted to get rid of the crystal so badly he would've paid Aunt Hattie to take it. Finally, she did and the weird old guy left. But before he walked out, he turned and gave my aunt a warning.

"Put the shape-shifter away," he said ominously. "And do not try to use its powers."

Aunt Hattie looked at the crystal and shrugged. It looked harmless enough. Still, I was kind of glad when she decided to put it in her safe.

But the next morning, when Aunt Hattie went to the safe to get some money, she noticed that the crystal was gone. She asked Jeremy if he knew anything about it, and he didn't even try to hide the fact that he had stolen it. He just took it out of his pocket, grinned, and said, "It works. Watch."

He looked around the room and finally rested his devilish expression on Puffin, Aunt Hattie's tabby cat. All of a sudden, Puffin wasn't a cat anymore. She was a huge, grotesque rat, with filthy, mangy fur. Fleas were swarming all over poor Puffin, and she was squealing and biting at her own flesh.

"Stop it!" screamed Aunt Hattie. "Jeremy, what are you doing? Puffin is just a harmless cat!"

Jeremy shrugged. "Okay," he said. "I'm sorry. I wish I hadn't done that. I wish Puffin was back to being the same stupid cat she used to be."

The change happened so fast it was imperceptible. Puffin looked the same as before, except she looked a little confused and there were little red marks where she'd bitten herself.

"Give me that crystal in your hand!" yelled Aunt Hattie. "Give it to me this instant, or so help me, I'll call the police."

Jeremy just chuckled.

"I'll tell them you robbed my safe," Aunt Hattie threatened.

"What safe?" Jeremy asked, rolling the crystal in his hand.

Where the safe had been there was now a rolltop desk. The rolltop opened by itself, and inside, crawling all over papers, pens, and paper clips, were dozens of rattlesnakes.

Aunt Hattie and I both screamed. But the terror had only just started. For suddenly, the phone started ringing nonstop.

Jeremy looked at me and commanded, "Pick it up." And as if pushed by some unseen force, I did as I was told.

Instantly, as I held the receiver to my ear, the hair rose on the back of my neck. The voice on the other end of the line was my own voice, asking for *me*! I hung up, but that didn't stop my voice from coming loud and clear over the line, and it didn't stop the rattlers from slithering down the legs of the desk and coiling around my legs. In fact, the deadly things were popping up all over the shop, as if they were sprouting from seeds.

"Get rid of them!" demanded Aunt Hattie.

"Of course," said Jeremy. "Your command is my wish." He grinned maniacally and ordered the slithery things gone. Then he looked around. "I sure hope I got them all. I mean, I hope I didn't *forget* any. I'd hate for you to get into bed tonight and find you had one under your covers."

It was at about this point that my aunt started to plead with him. "Stop doing these horrible things, Jeremy. Don't you know that I love you like a son?" She burst into tears. "Why would you want to scare me like this? Why, Jeremy, when I've been so good to you?"

"It's fun," he said simply.

Aunt Hattie just about lost it after that. She kept after him for the next hour, begging with him one minute, telling him off the next.

Finally, Jeremy just sneered at her and said, "Dry up."

And that's precisely what Aunt Hattie did. Her skin became all dry and cracked looking, and pieces of it started coming off in flakes, like some kind of nightmare dandruff. Her whole body was affected, and she started scratching like crazy.

Then Jeremy turned on me. I could see by the look in his eyes that he was trying to decide how to have fun with me. Then he murmured, "I've got it," and began rubbing the crystal, his eyes widening with pleasure.

I knew he'd made his wish when I suddenly started to feel very odd, but at first I didn't know what it was he'd done to me.

"You look grubby," he smirked. "You need a shave."

I was confused at first, then horrified, as I put my

15

hand to my face. I was growing a beard! I ran to a mirror hanging in the back of the shop, took one glance, and just about went into shock. Jeremy had changed me into a man, complete with a five o'clock shadow.

Meanwhile, poor Aunt Hattie was too busy scratching at herself to notice what had happened to me. Her skin was all rashy, and flaking off in patches as she continued to scratch wildly, trying to get relief from the terrible itching.

Jeremy was laughing at both of us. Furious, I charged at him and tried to grab the crystal from his hand. But he tripped me, and I went flying.

Now crawling on my hands and knees toward him, I begged Jeremy to change me back to normal. Aunt Hattie, now in great pain, was also on her knees begging him to free her from the horrible itching.

"Sure, no problem," he said. "All you've got to do is never mess with the crystal and never say anything about what's happened."

We agreed immediately to his terms, and he stopped our torment. Then he tossed the crystal in the air and, catching it, said, "Of course, you've got to be *real* nice to me. If you're not, and you ever annoy me, then naturally I'll have to punish you."

*   *   *

For the last three weeks Jeremy has kept his promise . . . sort of. Sometimes he uses the shape-shifter to make changes to objects in the house—probably just to scare us. But at this point he actually seems bored with torturing us.

16

Mostly, both Aunt Hattie and I just try to stay busy and keep out of his way. He's disconnected the phone and closed the shop to customers. We've become his prisoners. In his warped mind he thinks he's cut off our every possible contact with the outside world. But I have one last hope.

In my pocket is a letter to the police. My only problem is getting it to them. It's all written, addressed, and stamped. I keep it ready at all times. All I have to do is get it in the little mailbox on the wall right outside the front door of the shop. It sounds easy enough, but if Jeremy catches me, I know I'll regret it.

I've concluded that the trick is to be patient enough to wait until he's distracted. I'm biding my time, because if I mess up he might even kill me.

Today Jeremy is looking out the window in the far corner of the shop, and there's a gleam in his eyes. He's clutching that miserable crystal, and I know he's up to something.

I peek out the window in the front door. At first I don't get it. Across the way is an apartment building, and a guy is walking toward the door. I've noticed him before, and noticed that his girlfriend lives there. The guy is all dressed up, and he has a bouquet of flowers behind his back. He's at the door now, knocking. And Jeremy is watching, chuckling to himself.

As the door opens, the girl comes out. But the look on her face is anything but happy. Instead, she looks horrified. When she actually starts screaming, I can see why. Her boyfriend has changed into a skeleton with rotted flesh and bits of ragged clothing hanging from his bones. And the flowers in his hand—they're as dead-looking as he is.

Jeremy thinks this is the funniest prank he's ever pulled. He's doubled up with laughter, and the girl is screaming louder and louder, like she's going insane.

But all I can think about is that now is my chance. Quickly, I slip out the front door, shove the letter into the mailbox, and put up the little red flag on top so the mailman will know there's a pickup. I'm about to creep back inside, when I feel Jeremy's eyes on my back.

"What're you doing?" he asks coldly. He's standing right behind me in the open doorway.

My mind is racing. *Did he see me drop the letter into the mailbox?* I wonder. *Should I make up some excuse or just play dumb?* I have no idea what to do except try to bluff my way through.

"I . . . I heard the screaming," I tell him, pointing across the way. "I went to see what was happening."

There's suspicion—*lots of it*—in his eyes. I don't think he believes me, but I also don't think he knows what I've done.

"Get inside," he orders.

I do as I'm told and slowly walk back inside. Shutting the door behind me, I go to a window and look back across the street. Jeremy, fortunately, is looking out another window and not paying attention to me. He doesn't want to miss any of the aftermath of his prank on that poor girl and her boyfriend.

By now, people have come running. The girl has passed out, but her parents are there, and she seems to be coming to. The boy has returned to his normal self— a nice-looking guy in a suit holding a bouquet of fresh flowers. The girl sits up, opens her eyes, then starts screaming again, and tries to get away from her boyfriend even though he looks normal. She just keeps screaming, crying, and babbling, and it seems like she's lost it. It'll be a wonder if she doesn't end up in a mental hospital.

Soon the show appears to be over, so Jeremy pulls the blinds on all the windows. He looks to where Aunt Hattie is frozen with fear in the corner, then he looks at me. It is a long, hard look.

"You aren't up to something, are you?" he asks me, coyly batting his eyes. "You weren't trying to get away from me, were you?"

Good, I think. *He's on the wrong track.*

"Are you sure you weren't trying to make a run for it?" he asks again, trying to trap me in a lie.

"No, Jeremy," I insist. "I wasn't." I hang my head for effect. "I'm sorry I went outside. It won't happen again."

"Forgive me for being so blunt," he says liltingly, "but I don't trust you." He giggles, and I can see he's thinking up some kind of punishment. He rubs the crystal in his palm. "You just make my flesh crawl. See?" he says, holding out one arm. Under his skin, I see long black worms crisscrossing and slithering every which way, making his skin ripple and spasm.

But I've seen so many of his sick tricks, I'm almost used to them. I almost have to pretend to be horrified.

"Oh please, stop!" I exclaim, putting on an act.

"Gross, isn't it?" he asks, wanting confirmation of how twisted he is.

"Oh, it's terrible!" I say, puffing up his dark little ego. Personally, I couldn't care less if he had worms crawling under his skin for the rest of his life. The important thing is that it's keeping him happy and, most important of all, he's forgotten about my being outside.

Now all I have to do is wait, hope my letter gets delivered, and finally escape this nightmare.

* * *

It takes three days, but the cops finally do show up. One's a young woman, who looks like a rookie, and the other's kind of an older-looking man, the grizzled veteran type.

Aunt Hattie's the one who opens the door to them, and she's totally surprised. Me, I'm trying to think real fast about how to handle the situation. I see Jeremy at the top of the stairs, and he's looking from the cops to me. He's probably already figured out what's going on, and that somehow I am responsible. But what move is he going to make? Is he going to do something to me, to Aunt Hattie, or to the cops? Or will he try some combination of all three? I have no way of knowing, and I prepare myself for something terrible.

But all he does is turn away and slink back up into the shadows. When I hear his bedroom door close, I run over to the cops, who are already asking Aunt Hattie about the letter. She's super nervous, and doesn't know what to say, so I tell them I'm the one who sent it.

"According to this letter," says the grizzled veteran cop, "there's a thirteen-year-old boy named Jeremy who's stolen some sort of a crystal." He raises his eyebrows. "And supposedly this crystal gives the boy some kind of power to terrorize you. Is that right?"

"Yes," I tell them, trying to be brave. "It's all true."

"Is the boy here?" asks the lady cop, a tall Latina.

"Jeremy is upstairs," I say. "But he's dangerous. You should call for backup."

The cops exchange glances. "No need for that," says the veteran cop, already headed up the stairs, with his partner right behind him. "I think you've been watching too much television, young lady."

Aunt Hattie and I follow them upstairs. We point out Jeremy's room, and the cops knock on the door. But there's no answer.

Aunt Hattie and I look at each other. "What's he up to?" I whisper. But she just shrugs and looks more terrified than ever.

"Are you sure he's in there?" asks the female cop.

I nod yes.

"And his name's Jeremy, right?" she asks.

I nod again, and she knocks a second time on the door.

"Jeremy," she calls through the closed door. "We're police officers. May we have a word with you?"

Still no answer.

Nodding to his partner, the male cop turns the knob and swings open the door.

Sitting on the bed in a tattered terry cloth bathrobe is a frail, wrinkled old man. He has a vacant look in his eyes, and his hands are palsied and trembling. Right off, I know what Jeremy's trying to pull.

"Who's this?" the lady cop asks me.

"That's Jeremy," I tell her. "But, see, what he does is—"

The other cop has a sneer on his face, and cuts me off. "*This*," he says, pointing to the old man, "is Jeremy—the thirteen-year-old *boy* you wrote to us about?"

"Yes, but . . ." says Aunt Hattie, trying to back me up.

Already the two cops aren't listening. They look at Aunt Hattie and me like we're nuts, and head out of the room, down the stairs.

The old man Jeremy chuckles. He is really enjoying this. Maybe just a bit too much for his own good.

I make a move toward him, but he catches on real quick to what I'm thinking. He reaches into the pocket of his robe and pulls out the crystal with a shaky, wrinkled hand. Then, in a quivering voice, eyes on me, he says, "I wish to change myself ba—"

But with all his attention focused on me, Jeremy's not ready for the karatelike blow from Aunt Hattie. She must have delivered it as if her life depended on it, because it is so strong I can actually hear the snap of Jeremy's feeble wrist bone as it breaks.

He screeches in pain, and the crystal tumbles from his hand. Frantic, he goes after it, but he's old and slow . . .*very* slow. In fact, I don't even have to move quickly to step on his hand and crush his scrawny fingers just before they reach his precious crystal.

I bend down and easily pick it up as he writhes in pain on the floor like the snake that he is. Holding the crystal tightly in my fist, I say loud and clear, "I wish this crystal would vanish forever!"

"What are you doing?" squawks Jeremy in his old man's body. "What are you going to do to me?"

"Nothing," I tell him.

"Please," he begs, "change me back!"

"With what?" I ask, and smiling, I open my empty hand.

CRASH SITE

"**D**ad, it's the twenty-first century! Why are there still wars?" demanded thirteen-year-old Randy Stack. "And why do they have to take you? I don't want you to go."

"I have to go, son," Mike Stack said, casting a sad glance at his young wife, Madeline, as tears welled up in her eyes.

"But, Dad, you won't come back," Randy pleaded. "I know it."

"Randy," Mike began, bending down on the tarmac of Morton Military Spaceport, in the California desert, to take his son in his arms. "Son, I enlisted. I didn't know there would be a war, but now one has broken out in Indonesia, and I have to go. It's my duty." He glanced over at the military air train being loaded on the runway, a super-train that would arrive in Indonesia in less than two hours.

"Your dad never came back from Vietnam," Randy

challenged. "And your grandfather never came home from Korea." He glanced up at his mother, now sobbing into a handkerchief. "I'm sorry, Mom. But Dad's abandoning us."

Mike Stack looked from his son to his wife. He could hardly argue with the boy, for he'd had a similar argument with his dad long ago, about how the men in their family seemed to go off to wars and never return. In fact, his great-grandfather, Randy's great-great-grandfather, had died in World War II.

Now, the engines of the air train, ready to whisk Mike off to Indonesia, came to life with a sudden earsplitting roar.

"Let's go, soldier!" an officer yelled at him.

"I have to go now," Mike whispered in his wife's ear. "I love you." Then, turning to his son, Mike nearly yelled to be heard over the roar of the engines. "I want you to be strong, Randy. And take care of your mom. Promise?"

Hanging his head to hide the tears in his eyes, Randy nodded, then looked up as his mom and dad kissed and hugged.

"Move it, soldier!" the officer yelled again.

And so, Mike Stack hefted his pack, then ran toward the waiting train that would take him off to war.

* * *

Sitting quietly, alone with his thoughts, as the supersonic air train whizzed along at an altitude of eight thousand feet, Mike kept seeing his wife's tear-stained face. He also kept hearing his son's words.

What the boy had said about being abandoned and what war had done to Mike's family, down through history right up to the present year, 2002, made Mike think.

His great-grandfather had disappeared on a helicopter flight during the Battle of the Bulge in 1944. Almost the same thing had happened to his grandfather in Korea in 1951. But Mike's keenest memories were of his own father, Thurmond Stack, who had fought in the war in Vietnam. In 1972, during a helicopter assault behind enemy lines, Thurmond Stack and the rest of his platoon had been reported as missing and presumed dead, and Mike had grown up fatherless. *Am I going to do that to Randy?* Mike wondered, watching the collage of browns, greens, and blues swirl by below.

The Supersonic X-19, the air train from the United States to Indonesia, came in at exactly one hour and fifty-eight minutes—less than two hours to cover more than nine thousand miles. They landed at the spaceport in Jakarta at 0-400 hours, four in the morning, and traveling by GRV, ground rover vehicle, they were at the Semarang fire-support base before dawn.

Mike had barely enough time to unpack and meet the other members of his platoon—Frank Bloom, Gus Perez, Arnold Tapia, Carl Davis, Will Colbert, and Danny Roeder—before he was suddenly thrown into action. Orders had come down that morning for an S-and-S mission, Search and Save, even before Mike had arrived.

"Move it, men!" shouted an overweight lieutenant, as Mike tossed his gear through the open door of the waiting Panther helicopter gunship, then scrambled in after it.

"Make room!" Tapia called out as Mike picked his way through the semi-dark interior of the jet-powered chopper. Finally, he found a spot between Tapia and Davis. He sat down and checked his H-77 laser assault rifle, then studied the faces of the other air marines crowded into the gunship. They were weary faces, grubby and stubbled with beard; and the eyes, hard and tense, were eyes that had seen combat . . . and death.

Suddenly, a wiry, gray-haired officer pulled himself through the door of the chopper. "Good morning, gentlemen," growled Sergeant Gus Perez, X-Ray Bravo's team leader. The sergeant's eyes scanned the marines packed into the chopper's gray-green interior. "It is time, gentlemen, to rock 'n' roll!"

The pilot, his mouth a crooked slash, his eyes concealed behind oversized aviator glasses, looked over his shoulder to Perez. Then he nodded to Perez's thumbs-up, and turned his attention back to the controls.

Instantly, the jet engine whined, then screamed to life. The rotor chugged overhead, it gathered momentum, and the Panther helicopter rose from the ground. For a moment the Panther hovered, then suddenly leaning to one side, it slipped through the sky, whizzing briefly over farmland, a patchwork landscape of different shades of green.

"Listen up!" ordered Perez, shouting to be heard over the steady whooping sound of the chopper blades. He grabbed a canvas strap to steady himself. "Yesterday, at 0-900 hours, on a routine aerial reconnaissance flight, a scout helicopter's observer spotted something screwy in the jungle. A space in the vegetation displayed tree branches that were unusually straight and looked oddly like helicopter skids. On closer inspection, gentlemen, it was confirmed that it was indeed a downed chopper. Although no one in the region reported a missing aircraft, we're on our way now to take a look and see if there are any survivors. I will brief you further once we approach the crash site." Perez again scanned the men under his command. "Are there any questions, gentlemen?"

Everyone looked at each other, but no one spoke. Perez nodded to the men, then edged into the cockpit and sat beside the pilot, feeding instructions into the man's ear. Immediately after, the chopper rocketed on a line toward the ominous black-green humps of a low-lying mountain range.

Silence settled over the men. It was a time for reflection, for nervous fidgeting, and for checking and rechecking equipment. Bloom, his expression a taut mask of anxious anticipation, kept licking his dry lips. Colbert chomped on what appeared to be a whole pack of gum stuffed into his face. Davis and Roeder studied reconnaissance photos. And Tapia closed his eyes, leaned back against the vibrating metal wall of the chopper, and tried to nap.

Mike stared off into space. He saw his wife Madeline, and his heart ached for her. Then, in his mind's eye, he saw Randy. Tears stained the boy's cheeks, and his eyes were filled with fear and pain. Mike thought back to when he had been just a child, a little younger than Randy, and he was waving good-bye to his father. He remembered crying, as Randy had done, not wanting his dad to leave him, not understanding why he had to go . . . and suspecting, as Randy had, that he would never see him again. So clearly, and with such pain, he remembered growing up without a dad. The heartache was nearly unbearable then, and even now, as an adult, it was still with him.

Mike's legs began to go to sleep. He stood up and grabbed onto a steel support beam. Craning forward, he could see over the door gunner's shoulder. A rectangular cutout of Indonesia passed below. There was a green field. Then a woman standing on a road. She looked up at the helicopter, at its laser-rocket pods and electric-spear launchers. Then she passed from view.

Mike sat down again, wondering what the woman was thinking as the craft that flew over her arced left, in slow descent.

Perez made his way back from the cockpit. "Your attention, gentlemen," said the veteran sergeant. "Our LZ, landing zone, is coming up. It is code-named Betsy, and it's about two kilometers—a little over a mile—from the crash site. Once we've left the chopper, it will continue on to the crash site and drop blue smoke to mark where the wreckage is. We will be evacuated from LZ Betsy at approximately 1400 hours. Check your timepieces, gentlemen, and lock and load your weapons. This land is not our land. It's the enemy's, and we may be getting ground fire as we go in."

Mike unhooked his seat belt and switched the selector switch on his H-77 to full automatic. As the chopper made its final approach, Perez and Roeder fired laser bursts into the brush below, raking the tree line with white-hot electric beams to eliminate any surprise attacks. Then twin ultrasound "shredder" guns opened up in the bow, creating a deafening rattle that reverberated through the entire chopper.

The Panther's downdraft intensified as it slowed its descent, and a wild, swirling storm of dust and debris mushroomed up and around the marines as they debarked from the aircraft. His helmet wobbling, his upper body weighed down beneath his titanium-fiber flak jacket, Mike followed the others and jumped.

"Go!" shouted Perez. "Go! Go! Go!"

The men dashed across twenty-five yards of open ground, then forged across a slow-moving, waist-deep stream. Slogging through the water, they fired their lasers into the surrounding jungle, ripping into the vegetation—and whatever else might lay within. Once out of the rank-smelling stream, they continued running some fifty yards into a dense brush. Then they stopped to slap fresh electrocartridges into their weapons and to catch their breath. So far they had been unopposed, with no return fire and nothing to fight but a small fire started by one of the gunship's laser blasts.

Perez scanned the sprawling, shadowy valley in the distance with his binoculars, and they all watched as the Panther fired blue smoke into the jungle, marking the crash site. "Move out," ordered Perez, his voice a rasping whisper, his eyes on the blue smoke curling up from the valley.

As the men pushed forward into the jungle, they found a trail, which broadened into a gloomy forest. Towering trees the width of telephone poles supported a vast canopy of leaves that nearly blotted out the sun, rendering all below them light, dotted shadows. The darkness and, even more, the silence, of the place was eerie and disturbing. Every footstep, every movement, every breath taken by the soldiers as they moved, resounded through the twilight world, giving them away and making them marked men to the enemy.

And the enemy was out there . . . somewhere. Neither Mike nor the others in the platoon needed an explanation of the danger they were in. They all knew that below ground, in all probability, was an intricate maze of tunnels. In them, only a single sniper might be hiding, or, just as likely, hundreds—waiting to attack from the rear. Though cleverly concealed, and nearly invisible to the untrained eye, these tunnels didn't get past the veteran Perez. Again and again he spotted the entrances to possible tunnels and pointed them out, sending fear into everyone's heart every time he pointed his rifle.

Cautiously, Mike and his comrades crept along, some straight ahead, aiming their weapons forward and side-to-side, while others walked backward, their weapons guarding the rear of the platoon.

They left the green cathedral of trees and began their descent down a steep hillside, sliding and stumbling through the endless clog of vegetation that filled the valley. Hacking away with machetes, sweating profusely in the strength-sapping heat, they came upon the crash site with quiet surprise.

The downed craft was an AH-S Cobra helicopter, a relic of a bygone era. Where the lasers and ultrasound shredder guns should have been, there was only an antique mounted machine gun and automatic grenade launcher.

"Man, what is this thing?" asked Colbert, his words rendered almost totally inaudible by all the gum in his mouth. "Judging by the looks of it, I'd say this bird's been here a long time."

On the alert for the enemy, the men carefully moved around the upside-down helicopter and examined it. Mike, in particular, wondered about the age of the craft and what appeared to be a huge anthill inside the pilot's small, cramped forward area. He leaned in through the glassless window and, on closer inspection, realized that the "anthill" was a brown, decayed skeleton with ants trailing in and out of the broken, exposed skull. A splintered tree grew through the pilot's back where it had pierced him on impact.

Gasping in horror, Mike turned away, but then, drawn by curiosity—or something darker—he took a second and closer look. Once again, he peered inside the destroyed cockpit, this time seeing the remnants of two more skeletons that lay moldering in moss, slime, and stagnant pools of rainwater behind the pilot's seat. A fourth soldier, obviously the weapons control man, the gunner, had been thrown free. Rotted fragments of his uniform and flight helmet lay scattered on the jungle floor.

Perez, who had walked up behind Mike to take a look, removed his helmet and ran his fingers through his thinning hair. "Doesn't make any sense," he said. "The uniforms on these bodies . . . they're not modern fatigues. They're standard issue from about the time I was a seventeen-year-old private."

Unspeakable dread spread through Mike's entire being. He crawled into the body of the helicopter through the gunner's door, and climbed over the remains of the soldiers in the rear of the craft. His hands trembling, he moved over to look more closely at the skeleton in the pilot's seat.

Perez shook his head in disbelief. "I just don't understand it. This Cobra's the type of chopper we used in Vietnam. The headgear, the uniforms, and even the weapons—"

He was cut short by a low, gurgling cry coming from inside the chopper, and a moment later Mike Stack appeared in the door. From his hands dangled a set of dog tags he'd removed from the body in the cockpit. His face was slack, pale, numb looking. "Th . . . these tags," he stammered. "They . . ."

Suddenly, a powerful explosion shattered the world around them, puncturing metal, shredding vegetation, and spattering muddy earth in every direction. Everyone dove for cover . . . or collapsed in a heap. It was as if the jungle had sprouted with the enemy, and from it came hissing blasts of deadly light from lasers.

Mike rolled, and came up on one knee behind a gnarled tree. He fumbled with his H-77, and managed to flip off the safety. But before he had a chance to fire, searing explosions of light erupted all around him. Screaming, he dove face-first for cover.

For a moment there was silence, a stillness that was almost more frightening than the noise of gunfire. Mike raised his head slightly and saw a horrible collage take form before his eyes—all of it simultaneous and seemingly in slow-motion. A lone enemy soldier rose from high grass, hoisting the tube of a hand-held electrorocket launcher. He fired it just as Perez tossed a magnetic fire-fusion grenade. The jungle and the ancient helicopter flamed red in the same instant, rocked by separate but seemingly identical explosions.

"They're all dead!" Colbert was screaming in Mike's face.

Numb, Mike looked at him. The lanky little man had seemed to float out of the black smoke roiling up from the burning remains of the helicopter. And now he was pulling on Mike's arm.

"We gotta get outta here!" Colbert screamed, chewing madly on his huge wad of gum. "Perez, Bloom, Tapia—they're dead, man!"

A laser blast kicked up a glob of mud. Another zapped a black scar across a fallen tree. In the jungle, those of the enemy who had survived Perez's grenade were lumbering forward, firing their lasers at Mike and Colbert.

"I don't understand!" screamed Mike.

He continued to scream as he retreated. He threw down his weapon and ran blindly, stumbling after Colbert through the jungle.

"Shut up!" yelled Colbert. "Just run!"

The two smashed through the thick vegetation, the enemy in pursuit. Overhead and all around, beams of white-hot light incinerated leaves, sliced off branches, and punched flaming holes in the trunks of trees. Colbert suddenly tripped and fell. Mike dragged him to his feet, and in one swift motion the two were running again. They skidded down a slick embankment, then stumbled their way through high, wet grass. Soaked, they burst into a clearing as the Panther gunship streaked down from overhead, pouring out burning streams of laser fire into the jungle in an effort to cover the two madly scrambling marines. Then the craft made a sweeping arc and came back, hovering inches above the ground.

"Move it! Move it!" screamed the door gunner.

Seconds later, with Colbert and Mike aboard, the gunship throttled up. Drifting left, it clipped treetops, then steadied before rocketing up into the bright blue sky.

From the breast pocket of his fatigues, Mike pulled out the dog tags. "Stack, Thurmond," he muttered. "L-905-jn—PT."

"What?" asked Colbert, seeing Mike's furrowed brow. He wiped a smear of mud from his face. "Whose are those, man?"

"My father's," Mike said flatly. "He was in that chopper."

Colbert shook his head. "You're nuts, man!"

Mike stared at him blank-faced. "Those were my father's remains, and that was the helicopter he was in when he got shot down in Vietnam."

"Look, Mike," Colbert said softly, trying to reason with him. "That was a different war. It was thousands of miles from here and over three decades ago."

For a long moment Mike silently stared at the dog tags. Then he looked at Colbert. "Was it really a different war?"

"What do you mean?"

"Are any of them different?" Mike asked. "What if they're all just one long—"

But Mike didn't have time to finish his thought. A violent, hissing blast wracked the belly of the helicopter. He glanced over his left shoulder, out of the gun port, to see white smoke burst forth from an engine vent. The chopper coughed and weaved high, as the pilot fought to gain control. Below, the dark jungle loomed up. Mike saw lasers spear up at them from the ground, and in the next instant, a string of smoking punctures suddenly appeared in the glass of the cockpit dome. As if in slow motion, the pilot slumped forward, a smoking gash in his flight helmet. Not a sound came from the man. He simply nodded forward, as if dozing off to sleep.

"We're going down!" yelled the door gunner.

Acting quickly, Mike dragged the pilot back into the bay, then struggled to get behind the controls of the downward-spinning copter. Oil spattered the dome, and black smoke and red flames streamed from both engines.

"No!" cried Colbert. "No! No! No!"

Mike screamed, too, and then let out a bleating sob, as the jungle rushed up to greet the falling chopper. And then, suddenly, the engine died, and the wounded aircraft plunged straight down, like a dead weight, into the valley, breaking apart on impact as it hit the treetops.

Colbert, hugging the body of the dead pilot, was killed instantly in the jarring collision. The door gunner was thrown free, and fell to his death on the jungle floor. Mike Stack, in the pilot's seat, was pierced on impact by a tree—which over time would continue to grow through the bones in his back.

* * *

Ten years later Randy Stack, now a veteran soldier at age twenty-three, was piloting a Zodiac 9-11 chopper over the war-ravaged highlands of India. Glancing out of the cockpit window, he noticed something odd in the jungle below. A space in the vegetation displayed tree branches that were unusually straight and looked oddly like helicopter skids . . . .

LIKE MOTHER, LIKE DAUGHTER

*T*he weekday routine began . . .

Leona Benzinger was up promptly at 6:00 A.M., but she stayed in her room, wearing her bathrobe and an old-fashioned nightcap. She watched the clock beside her bed and, at exactly 6:15, she knocked on the wall.

"I'm up, Mother," her daughter, Joanne, called from the next room.

Then came the sounds of Joanne getting ready for school, after which, as always, Leona heard Joanne say, "I'm leaving now, Mother," through the closed door.

"Have a nice day, dear," Leona automatically answered, then she listened for Joanne's light footfalls as she walked down the stairs.

After the front door creaked open, then shut with a bang, Leona Benzinger went to the window and watched her daughter walk away from the house carrying a tote bag full of books. "Good girl," she whispered, happy to see that Joanne had worn her heavy coat against the autumn chill.

Enjoy your freedom while you can, Leona thought sadly, as Joanne headed up the street. *It won't last much longer.*

She dressed in an old woolen sweater, tattered jeans, tennis shoes, and a stocking cap. Then she went downstairs, ate a simple breakfast, turned on the television—more for company than anything else—and started her day's cleaning. As she worked, the thought struck Leona that she wished the house were larger, not because she needed the room, but because it would give her more to clean. In fact, she wished her house was endless, with room after room to be tended to. She liked cleaning. It gave her something to do and helped to ease the emptiness in her life.

Briefly, she entertained the thought of going outside, of cleaning up the yard, or going for a walk in the park. But the thought, like any thoughts of leaving the house quickly vanished. Leona Benzinger, forty-eight years old, had not set foot outside her door in eleven years.

*   *   *

Smiling was not something fourteen-year-old Joanne Benzinger often did. But a secret little grin was on her face as she walked home from school that day, and there was a lightness to her step that usually wasn't there. A boy had asked her to the Oktoberfest Dance. True, Edwin Nelson wasn't the Hunk of the Month. In fact, he was shy, awkward, and, probably in most people's eyes, unattractive. But Joanne identified with Edwin. Like her, he was a social outcast, a nerd, a loser.

Still, Edwin was sweet. He was nice to Joanne, and didn't seem to mind her dowdy clothes, mousy brown hair, and makeupless face. Unlike the other kids, Edwin didn't tease her. And most important of all, he didn't ask questions about her mother, the town oddball.

As Joanne turned the corner at Trenton Boulevard, the street where she lived, her pace slowed. Then, when she reached her house, she stopped dead in her tracks in front of it, suddenly not wanting to go in.

The smile now gone from her face, Joanne gazed at the dilapidated two-story home. Towering junipers and untrimmed oleanders swayed in the cool, mid-autumn breeze, slapping and grinding against windows covered with grime. Great rounded clumps of Bermuda grass had sprouted through a screen that had fallen on the ground.

My house looks like it has a skin disease, Joanne thought, staring at the holes in the white-painted stucco and the pieces of peeling paint that hung from the rotting wood over the doorway. Then suddenly from the upstairs bedroom—her mother's bedroom—a window opened with a screech.

"Why are you standing out there in the cold?" her mother demanded, gazing down at her.

"Sorry," said Joanne. "I . . ."

"Well, get the mail and come inside already."

Obediently going to the mailbox, Joanne flipped open the lid and found the monthly check from her father amid junk mail. Then she hurried up the cracked, puzzle-piece walkway and into the house.

The place, as usual, was dark, dreary, and horrid—but also neat as a pin, and very, very clean—a complete contrast to the disarray shown to the world on the outside. Also as usual, the place reeked of polish, wax, and disinfectant.

Sighing, Joanne neatly placed her tote bag full of schoolbooks and homework on the kitchen table. Next to it she set down the mail. She was hungry and wondering what there was to eat, when she heard an upstairs door open and her mother making her way downstairs. Involuntarily, Joanne's heart froze. *What does she want?* her mind raced. *She practically never leaves her bedroom.*

"How was school today, dear?" her mother called from the bottom of the stairs.

"Fine, Mother," Joanne said in the usual clipped tone she used with her mom.

As the odd woman shuffled toward her for a home-coming kiss, Joanne felt like running. Instead, she recoiled inwardly from the peck on the cheek, feeling a wave of revulsion. *Why does she have to dress like that?* Joanne wondered, looking away from the woman's weird stocking cap, the frumpy homemade dress, and grungy tennis shoes.

"How about a snack, dear?" asked her mother, at least *sounding* like a normal mom.

Joanne nodded and sat down at the table as her mother fussed about in the kitchen, eventually setting milk and a plate of gingersnaps in front of her. "Now don't make a mess, sweetheart," she said, like she *always* did.

Why not? Joanne thought bitterly. *Isn't cleaning what you live for?* But instead she said, "I'll be careful, Mother. Don't worry."

Her mother nodded approval, popped open the envelope from Joanne's father, glanced at the check inside, then carefully folded it and put it in her pocket. Joanne's father had left in the middle of the night about ten years ago. Everyone in town said that's what probably drove her mother to be the way she is. But why he left exactly, Leona Benzinger wouldn't say. As long as he sent his monthly checks, she was happy.

"Mother . . ." Joanne began, "a boy invited me to the Oktoberfest dance at school. And I was wondering if—"

"The answer is no," her mother said firmly. "Why ask a question when you already know the answer?"

"But, Mother, he's really nice. His name's Edwin. He's smart and I just know you'll like him . . . really."

"I won't like him at all."

"But why?" Joanne asked adamantly, determined not to just give up as she had so many times before.

"Because I'll never meet him—and *you* will never go out with him."

"Please," begged Joanne. "The dance only lasts until 11:00, and I'll be home by midnight. I promise."

For a moment there was an almost sympathetic look in her mother's washed-out blue eyes. "I understand you're growing up, dear. It's normal for you to want to go to dances and such things, but . . ." She stopped for a moment and began playing with a ringlet of gray hair protruding from her stocking cap.

"Then I can go?" Joanne asked, her palms sweating.

"I'm afraid not."

"But why?" Joanne nearly screamed, tears welling up in her eyes.

"Because it will only lead to heartache later on."

"But—" sputtered Joanne. "I . . . I . . ."

"Be sure to clean up after yourself when you're finished eating," her mother said coldly. And with that, she turned her back on her heartbroken daughter and headed upstairs.

* * *

The next day, at lunchtime, Joanne told Edwin she would love to go to the dance with him.

"That's great!" exclaimed Edwin, practically beaming with delight.

"Well, I, uh, gotta go," she said, smiling awkwardly. "See ya." She waved good-bye and hurried away, not feeling an ounce of guilt for disobeying her mother.

But during her last two classes of the day, Joanne started to feel a headache building inside her skull. It grew so severe that she was beginning to think that maybe she *was* guilty, so guilty that she'd given herself a headache. In fact, her throbbing head was getting in her way whenever she tried to think about what she might wear to the dance, or when she tried to plan how she was going to get away with going in the first place.

The dance was informal, which would make it easier than if she had to think about a fancy dress and shoes. She could get by wearing blue jeans, loafers, and a sweater—clothes that "normal" kids wore. Her hair, though, Joanne knew she'd have to do something nice with—something simple, maybe putting it up with a barrette or a ribbon.

As for getting to the dance, Joanne already told Edwin

that she'd meet him there. Her plan was to simply sneak out her bedroom window and climb down the trellis. The fact that her mother spent most of her time in her bedroom gave Joanne an advantage. *What am I worried about?* she thought, rubbing her pounding temples. *My mom never leaves her room. I can probably leave the house and come back without her ever even knowing I've been gone.*

And so, in preparation for her big event, Joanne bought lipstick, eyeliner, and mascara, and even a little bottle of inexpensive perfume from the drugstore on her way home from school. That night, in her room, she practiced putting on the makeup.

"I'll never get it right," she said, frowning at her face in the mirror above her dresser. She realized how clumsy and totally inexperienced she was at things all the other girls had learned from each other at school. *Well,* thought Joanne, *they have older sisters, or "normal" mothers who they can ask for help.*

Suddenly her door opened. Joanne frantically tried to wipe off the lipstick, but before she finished, her mother stepped into the room.

"Do you think I'm not aware of what you're up to?" her mother asked, bitterly. "Do you think I don't know the ways of girls your age?"

"I want to go to the dance!" Joanne said defiantly. "I'm not your prisoner. I have a life. Why do you want to make me like . . . like you?"

"I'm sorry, sweetheart, but I can't let you go."

"Why?" Joanne asked, stamping her foot.

"Unfortunately, you'll know why, and all too soon."

"What's that supposed to mean?" Joanne asked, growing angry now.

For a moment, her mother looked flustered. Then she grabbed a tissue off the dresser and handed it to Joanne. "Clean up your face," she said sternly. "You're not going to the dance and that's final."

I can't stand it anymore! a voice in Joanne's head screamed as her mother turned and left the room. *I'm not going to live like a freak, or be a freak, like her!*

For a moment, her father's face and voice drifted into her memory. She saw a chubby, pleasant man. And there was his laugh, so soft and gentle. Legos, she remembered playing Legos with him—and her mother. She was different then, when Joanne was a little girl. She was normal.

Then suddenly everything changed. Joanne had been four, about to turn five; that's when her mother's horrible screaming had begun. Had they been screams of pain or anger, or those of a woman gone mad? Joanne didn't know. She only knew that they had driven her father from the house. She also knew that right around that time her mother stopped going outside and started wearing odd clothes—weird hats and scarves especially—anything that would keep her head covered, even indoors. And in this strange, dark environment, Joanne had grown up, her mother's eccentric ways dominating—and warping—every aspect of her life.

"Well, it's going to stop right now!" Joanne resolved, wiping off the lipstick, then reapplying it more carefully. "I'm going to start acting normal from now on, even if my mother isn't."

She smiled at her reflection in the mirror. The face that looked back at her wasn't so bad. It was, well, almost pretty, Joanne had to admit, and there was something very new about it, too. Now there wasn't just makeup on her face, there was a look of determination as well.

* * *

The next morning, Joanne woke up feeling ill. She had a fever and a worse headache than the day before. The following day, she felt even worse, and although she wanted to go to school, if only to get out of the house, she was just too sick to get out of bed.

Her mother, who brought her tea and light meals, didn't look worried at all. In fact, she didn't even call a doctor.

But by that afternoon, Joanne was in agony. It was as if the back of her head would explode. "Please, Mother," she said, weak with pain. "Please call a doctor."

"Doctors can't do anything for you," said her mother matter-of-factly. "They can't change heredity."

"What are you talking about?" cried Joanne. "I can't stand the pain! *Do* something!"

"There's nothing I or anyone else can do, dear. It's simply a matter of genetics."

"Genetics?" Joanne whispered. "Am I dying?"

"No, you're not dying. It's just that the same thing that happened to me and that happened to my mother is now happening to you. Actually, I was lucky. I got mine so much later in life that I thought maybe it wouldn't happen to me. I got married, and I'd already had you, before it started to happen."

"What are you talking about?" cried Joanne. "Before what started to happen?"

"Before I got my first . . . just like you're getting your first, now."

"My first *what*?" Joanne asked, afraid she was going to be sick. If her mother had it, she wanted no part of it.

But instead of answering, her mother slowly pulled off the knit cap she was wearing, turned around, and parted her hair.

Joanne shrieked in horror. At first she saw three, then two more, small blue eyes in the back of her mother's head. The five eyes, all hideous, all unblinking, stared back at her.

Sickened, numb with shock, Joanne jumped out of bed, and on trembling legs she tried to run. But before she even made it to the door, the world began to spin. Then everything turned black, as Joanne collapsed unconscious to the floor.

* * *

When Joanne awoke she was in bed, and it was night. The pain was gone, but she still felt dizzy and disoriented. Shaking, she got up from bed—but something was terribly wrong. She saw the opposite wall and, at the same time, saw someone, sitting behind her, in the shadows.

"Someday you'll be just like me," said the shadowy figure.

"No!" sobbed Joanne, recognizing her mother's voice.

In horror, Joanne prayed it had all been just a nightmare. She reached to the back of her head, and felt the eye, the same eye with which she could now see her hand. Gasping, she groped her way to the mirror, turned, and parted her hair. Then, with amazement and terror, she stared at herself with the eye in the back of her head.

"There will be more later," her mother said flatly.

The house echoed with Joanne's screams.

* * *

Joanne did not go to the Oktoberfest, nor did she ever return to school. Rumors began to spread about her all over town, just like they had about her mother, and kids would hurry when they passed by her house. The place gave them the creeps, as did Joanne. Sometimes they would spot her standing at a window. Why, they would wonder, did she and her mother always stay indoors? And why did she, like her mother, *always* have her head covered?

THE CAVE

"**M**om!" I yell as I come through the back door.

There's no answer. She isn't home yet, so I limp upstairs to the bedroom I share with my little brother.

The place is a total mess. Back issues of my favorite magazines, *National Geographic* and *Rock Hound*, are all over the place. On my bulletin board and under the glass top on my desk are pictures I've taken inside caves. Practically everywhere in my room, you can find rocks of every kind. Obsidian, rhyolite, peridotite—just about any rock you can name, I've got it. In fact, I know everything about rocks. I even won the science award from Yarborough Middle School for my experiment on magnetic rocks. You might say I'm kind of a rock freak.

My younger brother, Richie, is sitting on his bed, watching me with his big blue eyes. He's smiling, and I can tell he's happy to see me. I hate to disappoint him, but I have to.

"Richie, I have to go to the doctor with Mom," I tell him. "Sorry, but going to the cave is out for today."

His smile changes into a big frown, and he says something under his breath that I don't quite catch.

"Come on, don't be like that," I say, tossing my school backpack on my bed and sitting across from him. "Tell you what. Tomorrow's Saturday. We'll start out bright and early, and we'll go to Blackmouth Cave, just me and you. We'll head out before Mom and Dad even get up."

Richie smiles when I tell him this, but I can see he is still disappointed. He's wearing blue jeans, his fluorescent red nylon jacket, hiking boots, and the leather gloves I bought him. He's all set to go spelunking—cave-exploring—today, and he has probably been looking forward to it since early this morning.

You see, my brother and I are really into the whole geology trip—collecting rocks, panning for gold, the whole works. But our favorite thing is cave exploring. Since the accident when I hurt my leg, though, my mom and dad are real funny about letting us go out alone. In fact, they're really weird about it.

* * *

As I sit here across from my brother, my thoughts go back to the day of the accident. It happened more than two years ago. It was a rainy day, like it usually is in Oregon, when my buddies, Matt and Kirby, and I headed off through the woods for Blackmouth Cave. We were wearing heavy jackets, and our backpacks were filled with mineral hammers, flashlights, sodas, and enough stuff to eat for a full day of caving.

Richie followed us, acting all babyish and whining that he was old enough to go with us. But he was only seven at the time, so Matt and Kirby told him to beat it and go back home. He started to cry. Eventually we all gave in just to shut him up.

When we reached Splitnose Valley, we had trouble finding the entrance to Blackmouth Cave. None of us had ever been to it before, although we'd heard a lot about it. Finally, we found it, but the mouth of the cave was real low, just a narrow slit beneath a rocky overhang, and we had to slither on our bellies like snakes to crawl in.

Inside, though, the place was pretty big, and we all shined our flashlights ahead. Matt started making fun of my little brother, because all he had was this little rinky-dink, purple-and-black toy flashlight. Richie got all mad, and I thought he was going to cry again, so I put my arm around him and told Matt to back off.

Anyway, we headed into the cave, and at first it was kind of disappointing. There was a large area shaped like a figure eight, in which other people had obviously been before. In several places on the ground there were circles of blackened rocks, bits of charred wood, and heaps of campfire ashes. And there was all sorts of litter—matchboxes, soda cans, and coat hangers that had been untwisted so that they could be used for cooking hot dogs and roasting marshmallows.

We climbed up a high boulder and we found another opening, which led into what appeared to be a spiraling tunnel. I stuck my flashlight inside, directing the beam along the ground. I didn't notice any trash or footprints, so it seemed like not many people had been in there before.

To get inside this tunnel, the four of us had to squeeze through a long, narrow tube made of rock. It was tight at first, but little by little, it widened. We went from our bellies, to our hands and knees, and finally to our feet, and finally made our way down into a huge, awesome cave. The ceiling reminded me of a church, but it was all natural, made of all sorts of sparkly rock studded with long, fanglike stalactites. They kind of freaked me out, because I felt as if I were in a monster's mouth, a hideous gaping hole that could suddenly close down on us and crush us into nothing. The thought of being swallowed by a cave was definitely not my idea of fun. Below the stalactites were stalagmites, which were bigger and fatter. Most of these were bright orange, and reminded me of huge carrots pushing upward from the ground.

Kirby gave me a high five. "This is *soooo* cool!" he exclaimed.

"Sure is!" my little brother piped in.

Matt rolled his eyes. "*Sure is!*" he mimicked.

"Shut up, Matt," I said.

Kirby had already plowed on ahead, and the rest of us followed him, playing the beams of our flashlights across the slick walls. As we walked, the ground suddenly sloped down into another chamber. This place was even larger than the one we'd just left. The ground was different, too. It was softer, kind of like a carpet. In fact, it felt like we were sinking as we walked, sinking ankle-deep right into the ground.

Matt touched my arm, and I thought I heard him whimper. The beam of his flashlight moved back and forth across the cave floor, searching to find out what kind of goo we were walking in. And then, all at once, we knew.

"Gross!" we yelled in unison as Matt's light revealed that we were slogging through mounds of thick, soft, rank-smelling bat droppings. Instantly, we all aimed our flashlights upward toward the ceiling. We heard a weird ruffling sound and suddenly the ceiling seemed to be alive.

"You don't suppose . . ." Matt began, his voice dripping with fear.

It would have been better if he hadn't said anything. It wasn't that Matt had talked so loud, but because we were in a cave, his voice boomed as though it were shot out of a cannon. It created an eerie echo that reverberated up and down the cave walls, triggering a chorus of chittering squeaks and furious flapping sounds. In horror, we saw that the ceiling was a tapestry of bats. In one seething movement, the terrible creatures writhed all over the cave roof, making it look like dark rippling water.

"Oh, man!" Matt groaned.

Set off by his voice, a great big flock of them took flight, circling the walls as if to terrorize us. They were so black we couldn't even see them, but we sure could *hear* them squeaking and flapping just above our heads. A few of them buzzed right at us, attacking like furry bombers, and some of them actually did hit us, flitting their wings across our shoulders or grazing the backs of our heads.

Matt was the most frightened of all of us. He froze, while the rest of us dove for cover right into the disgusting bat goo we'd been walking in.

Still on his feet, Matt was jumping around and pawing at himself, trying to slap the bats away. "They have rabies!" he kept yelling. "We're all going to die!"

"Get down!" I ordered him.

But by then, oddly enough, all the bats were streaming straight upward. I don't know if they just went into a cave higher up or somehow they went out of the cave altogether. Anyway, we were glad they were gone, although Matt continued to jump around and scream about how he was going to start foaming at the mouth and biting people.

"Did anyone get bitten?" Kirby asked, wiping bat goo off his face as he got up with the rest of us.

Matt didn't seem to care about anyone but himself. "I think I'm okay," he said, "but I want out of here."

That gave my brother a chance to get even. "What's the matter, Matt?" Richie asked in a snotty voice. "Are you scared?"

"Shut up, you little twerp!" Matt sneered.

"Calm down, Matt," I told him. Then I shone my flashlight on the others. "You guys want to head back? It is pretty freaky in here."

"Doesn't bother me," said Richie, trying to sound cool. "I don't get scared easy." He looked right at Matt. "Not like *some* people."

"Yeah, right," Matt said, looking pretty bummed out at being put down by a kid almost five years younger than him. "I'm not scared a bit, you little nerd."

"Coulda' fooled me," Richie shot back.

Matt gave my brother a drop-dead look. Then he turned and aimed his flashlight into the depths ahead. "Let's go," he said, head lowered, as he led the way deeper into the gloomy darkness of the cave.

Like sheep, we followed, and now, as I look back on it, that's where our troubles began, and what eventually led to the accident.

As we walked along, the path angled downward. There were all sorts of weird passageways everywhere, branching off into directions all their own, then connecting back together again. Just ahead, I heard my brother's voice, as though he were only a few feet away, and slightly off to the right.

I was trying to catch up to him, following the beam of my flashlight and the beam of his. But his light looked really strange, like it wasn't connected to anybody—like it was floating through the air. I started to get worried. You see, it's hard to explain what it's like in a cave like that. Everything looks so nightmarish. Things that are close seem far away, then all of a sudden you find yourself bumping into a wall that was right in front of you that you didn't even see.

I yelled out to the other guys, and told everybody to wait up so we could get back together as a group. That's when I saw two flashlight beams in front of me, so I headed toward them.

I was on solid ground, looking toward the lights, when suddenly I found myself sloshing through water up to my ankles. Up ahead, there was a sloshing sound, too, and I figured the others were in the same watery mess I was in.

"Over here!" Kirby shouted. He aimed his flashlight up at his face, making it look all white and blue, like a corpse.

And that's when it happened.

Maybe it was Kirby's yelling, maybe it was just going to happen on its own, but that's when dirt and rocks started falling everywhere.

Kirby's face, still looking corpselike from his flashlight, looked blank and his mouth dropped open. For a second I thought the scream I heard was coming from him, but it wasn't. It was coming from my little brother. It was coming from Richie.

That's when I panicked and made a stupid mistake. I started running blindly in the direction of his scream. You see, even though he was a pest, he was my brother, and I felt responsible for the little guy. Anyway, as I was running, I hit something and fell. Immediately, a terrible pain shot through my leg, and when I tried to stand up, I realized the bone was broken just above my ankle. I took a step on it, but the pain was excruciating. I could feel my leg was all twisted, and I could hear parts of the broken bone crunching against each another.

"Over here!" screamed Matt.

I crawled toward his voice, then I felt Kirby's arm go around me. He helped me up, and together we made our way toward the sound of Matt's voice.

"Richie?" I called out, really starting to panic now.

"Down here," came his chirpy little voice. It came from the same direction as Matt's voice.

I was relieved. Richie was okay, even though he did sound a little scared. Still, where *was* he?

"Matt, are you with my brother?" I asked, as Kirby

helped me walk toward where we thought the two of them were.

"Yeah," he said in a strained voice. "We're right by you."

I aimed my flashlight all around and, finally, the beam fell on Matt. He was almost beside me, lying on his side. A little bit of blood was dripping down from around his eyebrow and, for a second, I thought his arm had been cut off at the shoulder. In fact, it looked like his right arm was gone altogether, but then I realized it just disappeared into a deep blackness.

I played my flashlight from his shoulder down the line of where his arm should be . . . and that's when I saw Richie. He had fallen into a gorge, and now he was holding onto Matt's arm for dear life.

I peered over and saw that Richie was standing on a little rocky ledge. That's all that was between him and a seemingly bottomless pit. With my heart racing, I asked him if he was all right.

"I'm okay," he said, panting for breath and looking absolutely terrified.

"I know you are," I said, trying to stay calm for both him and myself. "Now don't move. Just hang on and let us pull you up."

Matt and Kirby and I gave it everything we had, but there was an overhang where Richie had fallen, and it was impossible to lift him over it. What we needed was a rope, and some more people to help haul him up and over the lip of rock.

I reached down and grabbed Richie's arm. "Go get help," I whispered back to the other guys. "I'll stay here and keep him calm."

Matt and Kirby were gone for only a few minutes, when Richie started to shake real bad. "I think I see a better foothold," he said. "I think I can reach it."

I started to tell him not to move, but he was already going for it. That's when a stone gave way. It tumbled down into the darkness so far below that we didn't even hear it drop. But we wouldn't have noticed anything like that anyway—because that's when Richie lost his footing and was dangling in midair.

I grabbed his wrist tighter, and my grip was stronger and more secure than before. But the pain in my leg was becoming unbearable. It was getting worse by the second. I hoped that I could hold on until Matt and Kirby came back with help . . . but I wasn't sure. I wasn't sure at all.

* * *

Today I still get chills when I think about the accident in the cave. My leg still bothers me, but the memory of the whole thing bothers me a lot more. My little brother sits on his bed across from me with his big blue eyes. I can tell he's thinking about the accident, too.

Downstairs, the front door just shut, and I hear my mom calling me. She says it's time for my weekly appointment with Dr. Colby. *He's* the crazy one, you know. He insists my brother died two years ago, that he fell to his death in the cave.

THE TRAP DOOR

Some of the trees in the swamp on either side of the road were alive. Most of them, however, were dead, water-blackened skeletons of wood, standing up straight or lying on their sides in the foul-smelling, polluted waters of the bayou. The water, everyone in town admitted, was disgusting. A thick, lumpy skin of yellow muck lay on the surface, cooking in the Louisiana sun, and the water, littered with trash, was practically iridescent from the presence of petroleum and other chemicals, decades of spillage from factories and refineries upriver.

Through this wasteland, down a dirt road that bisected it, Jimmy Joe Gelber plodded along with all his earthly goods in his backpack. His shirt clung to his back, and his freckled face was shiny with perspiration. The sole of one shoe hung loose, like a mud-caked tongue, flipping and flopping with each step. His head lowered, his eyes on the ruined, annoying shoe, Jimmy cursed himself for running away from home. His shoe, the heat, and the chemical stench in the air, not to mention the mosquitoes that forever droned about his head, were all making him crazy.

"I should have thought this through a little better," Jimmy muttered to himself, thinking back to the stupid argument he'd had with his parents over not being allowed to go to summer camp. When they refused to give in, running away had seemed like the only option. At the time, the idea even seemed kind of appealing. It had seemed adventurous, fun, even better than going to summer camp.

But running away had quickly become something else for Jimmy, something not very much fun at all. It was only the third day on his own, and already he was grubby, miserable, and lonely, walking down a road going nowhere.

A clutter of dilapidated clapboard buildings loomed ahead, causing Jimmy to speed up his pace, in hopes of finding food and water, and perhaps even more important, companionship. Ever since Jimmy had left home, he had been filled with a gnawing emptiness. Now, as he came upon the ruined buildings, his heart sank once again, and he felt lonelier than ever.

The town, a tiny grouping of homes and small stores, was obviously abandoned. Almost uniformly, the wood structures sagged, warped and bleached by the sun and rotted by the ever-present moisture in the Louisiana air. A sign in front of the largest place, a combination house, store, gas station, and diner, promised Bait, Gas, Cajun Cooking, and Ice-Cold Soda Pop. Out of curiosity, and to get away from the blistering sun, Jimmy wandered into the place.

The first thing he saw was a rusted cooler filled with dark, stagnant rainwater. A flotilla of oversized mosquitoes nested on the surface, and a dead rat with tumorous growths on its belly floated upside down, half-submerged. Jimmy turned away in disgust. Then he jumped back, startled, as something let out a sucking *hiss* somewhere above.

Slowly, Jimmy tilted his head upward and gazed into the rafters. A cat, its fur thin and mangy, hissed again; the sound, lower in pitch now, had changed into an unearthly growl. Along a rafter, the terrible cat crawled on its belly, seeming to stalk Jimmy, ready to pounce, as the boy continued to retreat. Unable to take his eyes off the creature, Jimmy watched as the furry monster leaped from one rafter to another.

And then . . . it showed its other side.

Screaming, Jimmy ran from the place. He'd only seen it for an instant, but it was enough for a lifetime of nightmares. The cat had a second, undersized head growing out of the side of its neck!

"Oh, man!" Jimmy yelped, breaking into a run, ignoring the sole of his shoe that flapped madly as he fled down the road. He was sure that the cat was on his heels, ready to sink its teeth—*both* sets of teeth—into him.

He ran for as long as his breath would hold out. Then drenched with sweat, gasping, sucking in huge lungfuls of hot, humid air, Jimmy finally slowed to a trot, then to a walk. Cautiously, he looked back down the road. The cat was nowhere in sight. Still, he could hear something. In the near distance, screened from

view by dead and dying trees, something was coming—
a car or truck, its motor groaning and its springs
squawking. Finally, a pickup emerged around a bend.

"What y'all doin' out here, boy?" drawled a beefy,
big-bellied man behind the wheel, after the truck had
eased to a stop in the middle of the road.

"I . . . I ran away from home," Jimmy stammered,
still reeling from the image of the two-headed cat. "And
I don't know where I'm going, or, even where I am."

The man pulled a toothpick from his mouth. "A
runaway, huh?" He slid the toothpick back into his
mouth, his lips twisting up into a bemused smile. "Well,
you're welcome to a lift, if you want." He chuckled.
"Even if you don't know where you're headed, my guess
is this ain't nowhere you want to be. Am I right?"

"Yes, sir," Jimmy said, his hand on the door handle
of the old truck. For a moment, he hesitated.

Never take a ride from a stranger, his mom's voice
echoed inside his head. The warning was loud and
clear, but what could he do? He had to get out of this
horrible swamp. "Thanks for the ride, sir," Jimmy said,
sliding into the cab onto the lumpy seat. He settled
back as the beat-up truck rattled away, jerking and
bouncing along the rutted, uneven road.

The man squinted at the road stretching ahead, and
pulled down a dusty windshield visor against the glare
of the late afternoon sun. "What's your name, boy?" he
asked, the words whistling through his cheap, plastic-
looking dentures.

Jimmy told him, then reluctantly shook the long-
fingered hand, sandpaper rough with thick calluses,
that the man offered him.

"Evan L. Evans is my name," the man said, his oversized, bony paw of a hand still swallowing Jimmy's. "How old are ya?"

"Fourteen," Jimmy replied, finally pulling his hand away.

"Same as my boy," the man said, pushing up his loose dentures with his tongue. "Where are you from?"

"Baton Rouge, sir."

"Well, now, Jimmy Joe, you *are* a long way from home! What are you doin' way out here in this swamp?"

"Don't know for sure. I mean, it's like I just took off, and this is where my feet took me."

"Your folks know where you are?" Evan L. Evans asked, eyeing Jimmy carefully.

"No, sir."

Evans nodded, but made no comment. Then driving with one hand on the wheel, he looked back at the road, scratching a mosquito bite near the strap of his bib overalls.

For a moment, the two drove in silence, then Jimmy asked, "Do you know what I saw back a little ways before you picked me up, sir? Do you know what's in those old buildings back there?"

"Can't say as I do." Evans looked at Jimmy. "Just what did you see?"

"A cat with two heads." Jimmy announced, then waited for a reaction.

Evans laughed. "Lots of critters like that in this old cypress swamp, Jimmy Joe."

"You mean cats with two heads?" Jimmy asked in awe.

"No, what I mean is, all sorts of critters that got mutated. We have gators without tails, blind dogs, and animals born with no eyes at all. I'm telling you, I've seen birds without feathers, possums with six, sometimes eight, legs, and full-grown foxes no bigger than rabbits. And that cat you mentioned, I've seen it, too, a number of times. It's been hangin' around in Gautier Corners—that's what that town you came upon was once known as."

"How come the animals in this place are all messed up?" asked Jimmy. "You know, deformed?"

"Simple," Evans said, spitting out the window. "It's all the junk and chemicals pourin' into the rivers from the factories. Then the rivers dump their junk into the swamp, turnin' it into a sewer." He shook his head. "Any animal or plant life that doesn't die turns into a freak of nature now. And the people, it does them in, too. It makes them sick, sometimes even kills them, or at least drives them away."

"But you live here," Jimmy pointed out.

Evans tilted back a ratty, sweat-stained baseball cap. "Yeah, up the road a piece." He pointed a finger in the general direction of the dreary landscape ahead.

Jimmy pressed his point. "But how come you stay? I mean, you say it's so bad, and—"

"Got my reasons," Evans said sharply. "Got my family here, my wife, Annie Lou, and my boy, Simon, and they ain't about to leave."

"They *like* it here?"

"No, fact is we can't leave. Ain't got no other place to go."

Jimmy looked at Evans, then at the seemingly

endless swamp ahead.

"Nearest town is Prescott, some twenty miles up the road," Evans said, "but my place is coming up here on the right." He downshifted and braked to a stop where a side road cut a dusty scar into a grassy stretch of land. "Now, Jimmy Joe, you can try to hike to Prescott, though I surely doubt you'll make it before sundown. Or, if you want, you can stay the night with me and my family. I'll be goin' into Prescott tomorrow morning, and I can take you in then."

Jimmy looked at Evans, and felt afraid. He knew nothing about the man or his family, and the idea of spending the night with him or *them*, out in the middle of nowhere, had no appeal whatsoever. But then there was the road through the bayou, to Prescott. Even if he could walk twenty miles, who knew what mutants he might come across.

"Guess I'd like to spend the night," Jimmy finally said. "I mean, that is, if you'll have me."

"Well, then, that'll be fine," said Evans, already turning and heading up the side road. "The wife'll make supper, and you can help me with the chores, feedin' the animals and whatnot." He arched an eyebrow. "Now, helpin' out a bit, I would truly hope you have no objections to pitchin' in and givin' me a hand."

"Oh, no, sir," Jimmy assured him, a creepiness settling in his spine. "I don't mind helping out at all."

Within a few moments, a shack of a barn and a slightly tilting, whitewashed little house, set on stilts over the swamp, came into view through the trees. "Home sweet home," Evans muttered sarcastically, as chickens scattered away from his pickup. He stepped hard on the brakes and the truck's bald tires crackled to a stop on a driveway littered with thistles and dried-out snail shells.

"Help me unload, son," Evans said, motioning for Jimmy to follow him to the back of the truck where a variety of bags and boxes, supplies and mostly foodstuffs, sat in the bed of the pickup. Then, after several trips of hefting the heavy supplies, Jimmy and Evans made their way over the crunching shells to the house.

"My wife's not well," Evans confided to Jimmy, rapping his oversized knuckles on the door. "Annie Lou, we have company!" he called. "Open up!"

Hearing a cough and a rasping voice from within, Evans shrugged. "She must still be in bed." He fumbled for his key, then led Jimmy into the dim interior of the place. Behind sheets hung from the rafters, Jimmy could make out a bed, with the silhouette of a woman seated on it.

"Meet Jimmy Joe Gelber," Evans said, pushing Jimmy forward. "He's run away and will be staying with us a spell."

An odd, rasping titter erupted from behind the curtain of sheets. "Well, y'all are welcome, boy," said the woman, making no effort to show herself.

"Thank you, ma'am," said Jimmy, feeling peculiar and uneasy.

"Is Simon still out huntin'?" asked Evans, looking around.

"That he is," coughed the woman.

"Simon's my boy," Evans told Jimmy. "He spends most of his time in the swamps hunting, though pickin's have been kind of lean lately and . . ."

Suddenly, a commotion from below the floorboards distracted Evans. He snatched up a flashlight and grabbed a double-barreled shotgun from where it leaned against a wall and, kneeling down, pulled open a trap door. He handed the flashlight to Jimmy, who aimed it below, playing it over the inky, rank-smelling water that the house was built over. Water-logged, green-tinted wooden stairs led down into the water, and screening off the area below the house was a chain-link fence with a crude gate built into it.

"There's one!" Evans exclaimed, pointing.

Jimmy aimed the flashlight in the direction of Evans's bony finger, catching the glint of yellow eyes that belonged to a misshapen wet rat scrambling over floating debris.

Instantly, the shotgun roared, almost deafening Jimmy, and spattering the water with a pattern of pellets. The rat was gone.

"Stinking things," sneered Evans, dropping the trap door with a bang, then locking the latch. "Stinking rats get in under the fencing and disturb me and my boy." He tossed the shotgun onto a grimy sofa and headed outside with Jimmy on his heels. "It doesn't make a bit of difference how often I fix the chain links, they still get in."

Evans and Jimmy strode out onto a warped wood walkway surrounded by stunted pine trees. They soon came upon a crescent-shaped patch of soggy land, inhabited by a scrawny goat and a sickly assemblage of milk cows. From the chest of one of the cows, two extra, undersize legs dangled.

"Plum ugly, ain't she?" Evans said, shaking his head.

"Never seen the likes of a cow like her, sir," Jimmy agreed.

"I want to butcher her for meat, but Simon won't have it—she's his favorite." Scratching his scraggly beard, the man gazed out into the swamp, then turned his attention back to Jimmy. "I'll be wanting you to be feedin' this mangy bunch, boy. Okay?"

"Yes, sir," said Jimmy, his eyes glued to the hideous six-legged cow.

"Okay, then." Evans gave Jimmy a crooked smile. "Then fetch me four or five bales of wheat alfalfa from the barn, and a bucket or two of dried bugs and beet pulp. Then slop some of that in the troughs while I boil and filter some swamp water for them."

Jimmy nodded to Evans's demands, and strode off, glad to be away from the creepy old guy.

Instantly nauseated by the stench of rat droppings all over the barn floor, Jimmy nearly got sick from the even fouler stench of cow droppings that mingled with the rank, stagnant water in puddles everywhere. *How can anyone bear living in such a place?* Jimmy wondered, thinking of his parents and dreaming of his own home. True, his folks would be angry, and they'd probably punish him the second he got there, but that seemed a small price to pay for getting out of this wretched situation. Everything was spooking him, the six-legged cow, the mysterious Simon, Evans, and his wife, too. They were all weird. And what *was* wrong with Mrs. Evans? Why did she stay hidden behind the dirty sheets hung up in the house? Was she, also, deformed in some terrible way?

* * *

As dusk settled over the bayou, a steady, clicking sound of crickets and a guttural concert of croaking frogs rose around the odd stilted house where Jimmy worked with Evans. Ground fog was gathering, crawling solemnly across the lifeless water, and it all just added to Jimmy's uncomfortable feeling.

"Quittin' time!" Evans finally announced. The odd old man had been pulling bloated ticks from his cows then crushing them under his boot. In fact, the ground was now stained with splotches of black tick blood. "Let's get these critters in the barn so the gators won't be snacking on 'em."

Jimmy gathered up the buckets, and with Evans's help, herded the listless cows and one forlorn goat into the barn. Exhausted and starving, he followed Evans into the house, hoping that dinner would be ready.

Waiting for his eyes to adjust to the dim light inside the house, Jimmy glanced in the direction of the curtained-off area, where he detected movement behind the sheets.

"Y'all come out, now, Annie Lou," Evans called.

"Ya got the boy with ya?" she called back.

"That I do, Annie Lou."

Jimmy's heart skipped a beat and his palms began to sweat as the woman moved about behind the hanging sheets. Ugly visions of a woman without a face or some creature with tumors everywhere danced inside his head.

But when the sheet parted, only a skinny, tight-lipped little woman emerged. Though lethargic and pale, she seemed normal to Jimmy, physically, anyway. But there was an odd gleam in the woman's eyes. Scuffling along in carpet slippers, she approached Jimmy, and cocking her head strangely, she examined him, as though he were the most unusual thing she had ever seen. Then she pinched the flesh on his arm, as though to see how much meat was on his bones.

She's nuts, Jimmy decided. *What's she going to do, take a bite out of me?*

Then reinforcing his conclusion, the woman pinched and poked at his other arm and giggled to herself.

"Now, Annie Lou, don't pester the boy," chided Evans.

"Where's Simon?" she asked, squinting, looking around the little one-room place as though her son was somehow there but she just hadn't spotted him yet. "Simon!" she suddenly yelled, then went to an open window, scratching at the screen with broken nails, as she called his name again.

Taking her by the shoulders, Evans pulled her back, then guided her to a frayed armchair. "You just sit a spell, Annie Lou, and I'll see about supper."

"Uh-huh," said the woman. "Do y'all know my boy Simon?" she asked Jimmy.

"No, ma'am," said Jimmy, watching as Evans went to the window and called his son's name, his voice calling out across the darkening swamp.

"Be a nice surprise for him, you will," said Annie Lou. "Not many folks out this way, and no youngsters." She put a spidery hand on Jimmy's shoulder, causing him to wince inwardly. "Simon's the only reason why we stay out here. We just wouldn't feel at home anywhere else, and other folks would . . ."

But just then the sound of a gate squawking open under the house interrupted her. Then came a heavy splashing sound.

"What's that?" asked Jimmy, his flesh crawling.

"That's Simon," answered Annie Lou, kneeling down on the floor as heavy fists beat from below on the underside of the trap door. "Poor boy gets so impatient for his supper. Always so hungry, that young 'un is!"

"I don't understand," said Jimmy. "Why's he coming in from under . . . ?"

"How was your huntin', son?" Annie Lou asked, flipping open the trap door and letting it flop back with a bang.

The answer was inaudible.

"Not good?" Annie sighed. "Well, don't worry. Mama's got a nice surprise for her boy." She motioned Jimmy over.

Stepping closer to the trap door, Jimmy peered into the smelly depths below. Then he screamed at the sight of the monstrous face of Simon—a horribly mutated face, with glowing yellow cat eyes, and wild shocks of hair, oily and iridescent from the filthy swamp water. A gnarled hand with sharp talons reached up at Jimmy.

"Hungry, Simon?" cackled Annie Lou.

"Hungry!" replied the thing below, its voice a raucous squeal.

"Nooo!" cried Jimmy, as Evans's strong arms suddenly clamped hold of him from behind.

"Thanks for staying for supper," Annie Lou said, giggling as her husband picked up Jimmy and dangled the screaming boy over the open trap door.

"Feedin' time, Simon!" chuckled Evans, then let Jimmy drop.

Annie Lou slammed the trap door shut, bolted it, then put her fingers over her ears so as not to hear the terrible noises coming from below the house.

PIECE BY PIECE

I was ecstatic when my doctor released me two days early. I'd been in the hospital for over three weeks following my operation and, except for being bored to death, I was feeling pretty good. It took a bit of whining, but I was finally able to convince my parents and my doctor, Dr. Sanchez, to let me out of the hospital so I'd be home for Christmas.

Mom and Dad rented a hospital bed, which they set up in the family room. On a card table next to my bed, they laid out all the pills I had to take every day. They also set a little canister of oxygen attached to an oxygen mask by the bed, in case I needed it, and a phone so that I could call either of my parents on their beepers, or the hospital, if I wanted.

But I never used the oxygen, the phone, or beepers, even once. There was never a need. Like I said, I was feeling pretty good when I first came home.

* * *

Now, it's the third morning after Christmas, and I'm listening to my parents talk in the kitchen. Dad is cooking up one of his special omelets, and Mom—I can see her from where I'm lying in bed—is sipping coffee and reading the newspaper.

"Oh, that's awful!" she exclaims, looking up from the paper.

"What's that, honey?" asks my dad. He's out of sight, frying sausage in a pan.

"A woman from Newark, New Jersey, was found wandering and screaming in the woods. Her name was Teresa Ortiz. The corneas from her eyes had been removed. Yuck!"

"Removed?" asks my dad. "What does that mean?"

"It says here both her corneas had been *surgically* removed. And there's a statement by the woman that all she remembers was getting into her car." My mom starts reading directly from the paper. " '*A hand, with a strong-smelling cloth in it, went over my face, and when I woke up I was in terrible pain. I realized I was out in the country somewhere. I felt my face, and touched my eyes, and started screaming.*' "

"That *is* awful!" says my father. "Why would anyone do such a thing?"

"According to the police, they haven't got a clue yet as to the motive." My mom shakes her head. "I mean, there are all sorts of crazy people out there, and terrible things happen almost every day, but this is one of the worst things I've ever . . ."

All of a sudden my mom gets up and peeks in on

me. I quickly close my eyes and pretend to be asleep. I guess she got worried she'd been talking too loud and that I might have overheard.

Now it's a few days later, and I sure wish I didn't overhear, because I haven't been able to forget the story. In fact, I can't put it out of my mind—especially since today another sort of thing like it happens.

I hear about it on the six-o'clock news. This time, a man named Oscar Strom, a computer technician for a plastics company in Scranton, Pennsylvania, is the victim. According to the newscaster, Mr. Strom, thirty-one, was leaving work late one night when he was attacked in the parking lot by a man he described as being in his early forties. The assailant put a rag soaked with chloroform over Mr. Strom's face, and when Mr. Strom woke up he was in an alley, with strips of his skin removed, *surgically* removed, like Teresa Ortiz's corneas.

The story is supposed to be on the news at eleven, too, with further details, but I don't want to watch it. I've had enough, especially since I saw the police artist's composite sketch of the man believed to be the attacker. He looked average, like an ordinary guy, not the least bit evil or weird. He sort of looked familiar, even, but it wasn't a face I could place. It looked like it could have been anybody.

Once again I try to forget about the whole thing, but now that I've got the picture of that guy's face in my head, I can't seem to get it out.

* * *

That night, lying in bed thinking about it, I get real freaked out when I hear a knock at the front door. My dad goes to answer it. From where I am, I can't see anything, but I do hear two people, a man and a woman, who introduce themselves as police detectives. They ask my dad his name, then they want to know my mom's name, and even *my* name. The lady detective peeks in at me, but not before I quickly close my eyes. Then I hear her ask if there is somewhere private they can talk.

By this time, my mom has joined them. She sounds nervous when she asks what's going on. The male detective says something I can't make out, and then I hear my parents and the two cops go off to another part of the house . . . probably so I won't be able to hear.

I'm not exactly sure how long it is before the detectives leave, but it seems like an awfully long time. When they finally do leave, my dad goes with them. Then my mom, looking pale and upset, comes in to see me.

"What's going on?" I ask her.

"Oh, something to do with your dad's company," she says, a weird tone in her voice.

"What do you mean?" I want to know.

She doesn't look at me when she answers, and she stumbles over her words. Lying doesn't come easy to my mom. "It seems," she says, "that somebody at the company has been stealing . . . stealing money . . . you know, embezzling, and . . ."

"Do the cops think it's Dad?"

"No," she says flatly.

"Then how come they took him away?" I demand.

My mom's face turns all red and she fidgets with a tissue in her hands. For the first time I notice her eyes are puffy, like she's been crying.

"What's *really* wrong, Mom?" I ask, growing worried. "Did Dad do something?"

"No!" my mom nearly snaps at me. "He hasn't done anything at all."

I can see her gathering up her strength and trying hard not to let her true feelings show. I don't want to upset her any more than she already is, so I don't ask any more questions.

"It's nothing you should worry about, sweetheart. Really," she says, trying to sound convincing. "The police just need your dad's help in their investigation." She forces a smile. "Now, please, just relax and put the whole thing out of your head, okay? Will you do that for me?"

"Okay, Mom," I say, reluctantly.

She fluffs up my pillows and straightens the blankets on my bed. Then she hands me the remote-control. "Maybe there's something on TV you'd like to see?" she says, all cheerful, but I can tell she's faking.

I ask her what's on, and she starts looking through the TV program guide and reading off the shows. I channel-surf my way into a movie on the sci-fi channel, and Mom sits down beside me to watch, or, like me, just to stare at the screen, not really following what's going on. Our minds are definitely on other things.

Finally, I doze off, and when I wake up, another movie is on. My mom, however, isn't in the room. I hear her downstairs talking to my dad who must have come back while I was asleep.

* * *

In a few minutes, he shows up at my bedside and tells me a story that matches the one my mom told me. It sounds rehearsed, which makes me all the more suspicious. But I really get suspicious when the detectives return, and my parents start getting a lot of phone calls.

Whoever is calling, my folks want to take the calls out of my earshot. Also, my dad is suddenly staying home from work a lot, and he looks worried. And my poor mom is a basket case just about all the time lately. She never stops hovering around at my bedside, watching over me as if protecting me.

But the weirdest thing of all is the car I keep seeing parked across the street. I don't know if it's my imagination or not, but it looks like an unmarked police car is staking out our house.

* * *

Weeks pass and I don't see the surveillance car as much anymore. Mom seems to be relaxing a little, too, and Dad has gone back to work. Things seem to be getting back to normal.

Then one night my dad calls and tells my mom he's going to be late getting home from work. That really stresses her out. She locks all the doors and checks all the windows, like she's barricading us in. Then she roams nervously from room to room, as if making sure someone hasn't already gotten into the house.

Dad doesn't get in until almost ten. When he comes

through the door, Mom starts to cry, and Dad hugs her, apologizing.

"Tax season's around the corner, honey," he tells her. "I've got responsibilities, things I have to do."

"Things you have to do!" she yells, then storms out of the room. "Like what? What could be *that* important?"

"It's too complicated to explain," he says, sighing wearily, his face looking haggard and his clothes all rumpled.

I have trouble going to sleep that night, just like every night since all this weird stuff started happening. The next morning, I'm awakened by the television.

There's another story similar to the ones involving Teresa Ortiz and Oscar Strom. This one, though, happened in Middletown, Connecticut. A young man by the name of Peter Riley was abducted on his way home from watching a basketball game. In this case, the boy's right kidney was removed, then he was sewn back up and left at the side of the road. It sounded like some weirdo performed an operation on him.

But the difference in this case was that Peter Riley regained consciousness before being dumped. So, not only was he able to give a good description of the man who had abducted him, but he was also able to tell them a lot of other details. It was all real horrible stuff.

According to Riley, he awoke inside a motor home that was sort of set up like a small operating room. On shelves on the walls there were large specimen jars, inside of which were human organs—what appeared to be kidneys, skin, and a liver. There were also many photographs in the motor home of a young boy.

Still pretending to be unconscious, Riley reported that he was carried by the man out of the motor home and left in a ditch, where hikers found him early in the morning. He was taken by ambulance to a hospital, and said to be in stable condition.

* * *

That same afternoon, more detectives come to the house. A couple of them don't leave. Mom fixed up the spare bedroom for them. And through my window I can see two unmarked surveillance cars up the street.

* * *

The next day, police are saying they've made a major breakthrough in the case. They have a suspect, a man identified as Griffith T. Jones of Bismark, New Hampshire, a forty-four-year-old plastic surgeon with a history of mental problems. Jones's wife, according to the police, had divorced him in June, and she had been granted full custody of their fifteen-year-old son, Timothy.

But in early November, the boy had died in a boating accident, and over her ex-husband's frantic objections, the mother of the boy donated his organs. His liver had gone to a man in Florida; the corneas to Teresa Ortiz; his skin to Oscar Strom; his left kidney to a woman in Utah; and the right kidney to Peter Riley.

The police are theorizing that Griffith Jones had a complete nervous breakdown when his son Timothy died. Apparently, the man was even more upset that

Timothy's organs were donated without his consent. Further, the police believe that Griffith Jones, traveling in a motor home, is tracking down and abducting patients who received the transplanted organs. Insane with grief, Jones then surgically removes the organs, getting back his child, so to speak, piece by piece.

The police are still looking for Griffith Jones, but they don't seem to have any idea as to where he or his ghoulish collection of human organs is. Me, I'm terrified. You see, my operation last November was a heart transplant, and the heart beating in my chest is that of Timothy Jones. It's the one organ his father hasn't gotten back yet.

FORGOTTEN FIREWORKS

It felt funny to Jack Morley, a six-foot, two-hundred-and-thirty-pound man, to return to Lincoln Middle School. Funny to be around kids so little. Funny to be back at his old school, not to mention his last contact with formal education.

In the principal's office—Morley remembered *that* place well!—he filled out the job application form to be a bus driver.

Name: Jack Morley.

Previous Employment: Window washer, truck driver, house painter, and upholsterer.

Jack of all trades is what I should put here, Morley thought, chuckling to himself. Then he went on.

Education: Eighth grade, Lincoln Middle School.

Present Residence: 46 Carlisle Street, Odessa, Kansas.

Morley put the pencil down for a moment. *Boy,* he thought, shaking his head. *Not much changes, does it?*

He was thinking about how he still lived in the same house as he did when he was a kid, and how he still lived with his mother. He'd returned home after nineteen years on the road, drifting from one town to the next, from one job to another. Actually, ever since the eighth grade, his life had been kind of aimless.

Morley picked up his pencil. He had one more thing to fill out on the application. It was always the hardest—and the easiest—to fill out.

Criminal Record: None.

Morley always wrote that quickly and without thinking, always failing to mention the eleven people he had killed.

Signing his name at the bottom, Morley handed the form back to the principal and smiled. "I'm sure glad for this opportunity to work for Lincoln Middle School," he said, taking the principal's hand and shaking it a little too vigorously. "I sure like kids. Fact is, I still feel like one." He laughed nervously. "Yup. I still do."

And so, after the formality of filling out the application form, Jack Morley was told that he was Lincoln Middle School's newest bus driver, and that he started on Monday, the first day of the spring semester.

*　*　*

It was a bleak, cold morning, a morning that matched Morley's mood, when he first climbed behind the wheel of the big yellow school bus. Quickly, he glanced at the sheet of paper that showed him his route. It was a straight run along Platte Road, mostly through farm country, then back along Trinidad Pass, all ranch land, then down the long grade to Lincoln Middle School.

The oversized wipers slapped at powdery snow falling on the windshield as he pulled out of the fenced bus compound onto Platte Road, a dreary stretch of wet asphalt surrounded by snow-shrouded hills. It was cold in the bus, ice-cold. Morley flipped on the heater, and semiwarm air slowly began to flow into the boxy interior. The windshield began to fog up. He turned on the defroster, rechecked his route, then stuffed the paper into his shirt pocket. Squinting ahead, he spotted his first passenger, a scrawny boy with snow-flecked glasses that were rendered opaque by his steamy breath. The kid was wearing a huge quilted parka and his head was covered by a big hood.

"Morning," Morley said, trying to sound cheerful, even though he didn't feel that way. He *never* felt that way.

The boy, without answering, took his seat.

At Morley's next stop two girls, identical twins, were waiting, hunched against the cold, in identical red coats.

"Hello, ladies," Morley said.

Again there was no answer.

Rude little creeps, Morley thought, and drove on.

He offered no greeting at his next stop, but he received one, anyway.

"Good morning, sir." The voice was muffled, coming from a face wrapped crisscrossed by a scarf that was stiff with ice.

Where've I heard that voice before? Morley asked himself. He glanced up at the rearview mirror. The boy had unwound his scarf, and the face that was revealed was indeed a familiar one. It looked like one Morley had seen nineteen years ago, on a kid laid out on the grass in front of Lincoln Middle School, his eyes, glassy and staring skyward, unseeing.

A bit of uneasiness tugged at Morley's insides, but he shrugged it off and drove on.

By now, the two girls had removed their identical red earmuffs and had unwound their identical red scarves. The scrawny boy had pulled back his parka and was wiping his fogged-up glasses. Morley craned his neck and studied them in the mirror. Their eyes were fixed on him.

Suddenly, a sick feeling hit Morley in the stomach as he shifted his gaze from one face to the next, locking his eyes on each one in turn. He *had* seen these kids before, or so it seemed. And he'd known them, all of them, long ago.

It's just coincidence, he told himself. *Your mind's playing tricks on you.*

Though it was still chilly in the bus, Morley had broken out in a nervous sweat. Uncomfortable and feeling a bit light-headed, he opened the driver's window a crack to get some fresh air. But he was still uneasy, sweating like crazy and unbearably hot in his heavy jacket. Holding the wheel steady with his knees, he tried to wrestle out of the sweaty coat when suddenly the kids started to scream.

Startled, Morley grabbed the wheel, and almost went into a skid as he pulled hard to the right, narrowly missing a car coming in the opposite direction, its horn blaring, then fading away.

"You should be more careful!" yelled one of the girls.

"The roads are slick, sir," scolded another.

Shaken, Morley mumbled an inaudible apology. He gripped the wheel tightly, perspiration making his gloves feel slick inside. He wanted to take them off, too, but given the consequences of taking off his coat, he didn't dare. His head pounding, his neck aching from the tension, he scanned the road ahead for his next passenger.

Up ahead, he spotted a heavyset girl and carefully hit the brakes so that the bus came to an easy stop in front of her. She smiled and lumbered aboard. "Hello, Mr. Morley," she said.

"Huh?" he muttered.

"Hello, Mr. Morley," the girl repeated, wending her way down the aisle.

Morley swiveled around. "How'd you know my name, kid?"

"I have a good memory, sir," replied the girl, sliding into an empty seat in the back.

Morley fought the mounting terror within him. *Get a hold of yourself!* his mind screamed. *You're imagining things.*

Taking a deep breath, he punched the bus into gear. Then he engaged the clutch, and pulled away from the curb through a patch of wet slush out onto the road. Black clouds loomed ahead.

At his last pickup point on Platte Road, three kids waited for Morley. He remembered only one of them, Valerie Seymour. She had not only been one of the cutest girls at Lincoln Middle School, she had been the class clown. Her quick wit, offbeat jokes, and impersonations had driven her teachers nuts and cracked up her classmates.

"Oh, how exceptionally *rad*," intoned Valerie, hopping onto the bus, imitating Morley by using one of the trademark adolescent expressions he had been known for . . . almost twenty years ago. "It's Jack Morley, the world-famous bus driver." She snickered at Morley. "Who'd have thought you'd ever go so far in life!"

The kids laughed while Jack Morley cringed, his heart pounding in his chest. He was overcome with embarrassment . . . and mounting horror.

As he drove, his movements rigid and automatic, the names of former classmates started to flood back into his memory: Luke Benson, Paul Bellini, Annie Farber, the Hammond twins, Janet and Caroline. He tried not to think or remember . . . or scream.

Reaching the end of Platte Road, he swung the bus onto the road leading to Trinidad Pass, and entered a series of narrow, winding turns. He wanted to stop the bus, to get off, to run shrieking from it. Instead, frozen with fear, he relentlessly drove on along the now icy road to pick up his last passenger. He was pretty sure who it would be.

And there he was, just as Morley had expected, Randy Huff. The boy was in full view, standing in front of Huff's Quik-Stop gas station. Distance made the boy appear small, but he increased in size as Morley approached. Then Randy was big as life as the bus came to a stop, ice crackling under its huge tires.

"Hello, Jack," Randy said, climbing aboard.

The years hadn't changed him, or aged him at all, Morley thought. Randy still had the same unsmiling mouth, the blotchy acne, the watery, dark eyes, and the high forehead.

"Gonna call me 'Egghead' like you used to, Jack?" Randy asked, sneering.

Unable to speak, Morley's mouth fell open.

"Well, I don't know about you, but I'm glad to see you, Jack," Randy said, his eyebrows flecked with snow.

Morley fumbled for words. "What's going on?" he begged. "Come on, kids," he said, speaking into the rearview mirror. "I'm not moving this bus until I know what's going on."

"Don't you know, sir?" asked Valerie Seymour, grinning along with all the other kids.

Morley rose to his feet on rubbery legs and faced them. "Wh . . . what do you want from me?" he stammered.

There were no answers. Just private, all-knowing looks.

Morley's shaky legs almost gave way. "You're dead!" he screamed. "Don't you get it? All of you are dead!"

He ran from the bus, stumbling and sliding in the snow, and pushed his way into the phone booth at Huff's one-pump station. From a window of the house beside the station, someone gazed out at him, but he ignored whoever it was and frantically fed change into the slot. Trying to stay calm, he listened as a phone rang at Lincoln Middle School. Finally, a woman answered, and when Morley stammered that he had "an emergency situation," she immediately put him through to the principal, Isaac Whitson.

"Now calm down, Morley," Whitson said authoritatively. "What seems to be the problem?"

"It's a setup!" Morley blurted. "It is, isn't it?"

"What in the world are you talking about?" demanded the principal.

His lips trembling, Morley stared through the frosted panes of the booth at the faces in the frosty windows of the bus, some twenty yards away. "You know what I did, don't you?"

"No, I don't," said Whitson. "I mean, *is* something wrong? Did you have an acci—?"

Morley pushed down the phone cradle and hung up the receiver, cutting Whitson's voice in half. Then he dialed the bus dispatcher.

"I'm sorry, Mr. Zepeda's out of the office right now," said a sing-song female voice. "This is Ruth Miller, his assistant. May I take a message?"

"No, I mean . . . I don't know," said Morley. "See, it's my first day on the job, and I was sent on a run to pick up kids for Lincoln Middle, along Platte Road, and then . . ."

"But that's impossible," the woman interrupted. "I mean, there must be some mistake. We no longer have a run along Platte Road."

"What?" Morley gasped. He pulled the crumpled orders from his pocket, then read out loud. "It says here that . . ." He stopped himself. "South Platte Estates?" he mumbled. "But, I . . ."

"That's the new housing development," said the woman. "I'm afraid you misread your orders. I'll get hold of Mr. Zepeda as soon as possible and see what can be done."

Morley hung up. "Nothing can be done," he said to no one. Then he turned around. Valerie Seymour was standing right behind him. Her hair was burned off, and so were huge patches of skin all over her arms and legs.

"We gotta hit the road, Jack," she said with a snicker.

"No!" Morley screamed, trying to run.

But suddenly Annie Farber, her hair burned off and her skin blackened with soot, appeared out of nowhere and tripped him. He went sprawling, face forward, filling his mouth and eyes with snow. Rolling over, he blinked the cold wet snow from his eyes, and then the phone that Morley had just been using rang.

"It's for you," said one of the Hammond girls, the left side of her face badly blistered.

"Better get it," said Luke Benson, holes burned in his pants and shirt. His shoes looked all bubbly and melted.

Morley stumbled to the phone and pressed the receiver to his ear. From it came a chorus of screams, punctuated by explosions, the sound of fire crackling, and of something collapsing in flames.

"What's wrong?" asked Valerie Seymour.

"You've come back for me, haven't you?" Morley said, staring at the girl.

"For a loser like you?" asked Valerie. "No way!"

"Yes, you have," insisted Morley. "All of you have."

Valerie batted her smoke-reddened eyes, the lashes now stubs burned by flame and heat. "Well," she said coyly, in a Southern drawl, "I suppose anything's possible."

The others chuckled.

"I didn't mean for it to hap—" Morley began.

"For what to happen?" Valerie interrupted, feigning ignorance.

Morley licked his dry lips. "You were as much to blame as me. You were in class, and I was—"

"Ditching," said Annie Farber, finishing his sentence. "Tsk-tsk. Bad boy. You were a very, very bad boy. Snuck out of class, then came sneaking around outside the window. You looked like an idiot in the bushes, making faces at us."

"It was supposed to be a joke," Morley pleaded. "That's all."

"Great joke, genius," said Paul Bellini. "Tossing firecrackers into a classroom is real funny."

"I . . . I didn't think anything would come of it," Morley stammered. "But how was I to know that Egghead Huff was doing some kind of experiment with chemicals? How was I supposed to know the whole classroom would blow up?!"

"Everyone was trapped," said Paul, his voice hallow. "We were all screaming and begging for help. But what did you do?"

"You ran and hid, didn't you, Jackie boy?" said Valerie. "I was trying to get through the window, my clothes on fire, and the last thing I saw was *you* running."

"I was in shock," cried Morley. "I didn't know what to do, and I—" He turned and looked up at the sound of footsteps crunching in the snow. At first he didn't recognize the man. Then squinting, Morley saw that it was Wallace Huff, Randy Huff's father. Looking old and tired, his hands stuffed in the pockets of a sheepskin jacket against the chill, Huff made his way toward Morley.

"What're you doin' out here?" he called, still a few feet away.

Morley bit into his lip, and tasted warm blood in his mouth. "We're talking about the fire in science class, and about how I hid. I'm sorry, Mr. Huff," Morley cried. "It was an accident. I didn't mean to kill your son."

"*You* killed my son?" the old man asked, his eyes wide in amazement. "*You* killed Randy?"

Morley nodded and then started babbling. "After the fire department and cops got there, I went back to the classroom. It was still smoking and all full of water from the hoses. I was sure someone would point a finger at me, that someone had seen what I'd done. But no one had. And, like everybody else, I just stood there and looked at the bodies, laid out on the grass, some of them covered with coats and things, some of them not. I can't tell you how sorry I am, Mr. Huff."

Finally Morley stopped. With tears streaming down his cheeks, he looked at the old man, waiting for what, he didn't know.

Wallace Huff's face contorted with a mixed expression of disbelief, anguish, and contempt. He stepped closer to the distraught man now kneeling in the snow at his feet. "Look at me," he said harshly.

Morley looked into Wallace Huff's eyes.

"You're Jack Morley, aren't you?" the old man said.

"Yes," Morley said, coughing back sobs.

"Grown up, a man now, a pathetic man. And you're saying you were responsible for the fire that killed my boy?"

91

Morley could only nod.

Tears were welling in Huff's eyes. "And all those years everybody thought it was caused by something my Randy did. They told me that it was my boy's experiment that caused the explosion and fire." The old man spat on the ground, walked away, then walked back, looking Morley up and down. "And now you drive here alone, in a bus, to tell me *you're* responsible. Is this some kind of sick joke?"

Alone? Morley struggled to his feet. Where were the kids? He turned in a circle. The gas station was there. And so was the bus, parked at an angle over by the side of the road . . . but it was empty.

* * *

After Wallace Huff stomped off angrily, Morley stumbled back to the now-empty bus, and got behind the wheel. He released the brake, shifted into neutral, and took off. Not until he had traveled almost a mile down Trinidad Pass did he hazard a glance in the rearview mirror.

Sure enough, his passengers had returned.

Valerie, Randy, the Hammond girls, and the others sat quietly, gazing at him, watching his every move, their eyes seeming to bore holes in his back. The difference was that now they looked normal again, unhurt, unburned, like ordinary kids on their way to school.

Morley blinked, then looked again.

This time the kids' bodies and clothes were burned and they looked like the living dead. They were grinning at him. One of them stood up and came up the aisle. It was Randy Huff. He sat down in the seat behind Morley.

"How do you like the way we look?" Randy asked.

"Leave me alone!" begged Morley, his eyes staring straight ahead at the icy road.

Valerie Seymour instantly appeared beside Randy. *"Leave me alone,"* she mocked.

The others laughed.

Then suddenly Morley felt hands, Valerie's hands, clamp over his eyes.

She giggled as Morley tried to pry off her fingers, coming up with only the girl's ring. Bellowing with fear and rage, he fought her as the bus banged against the side of a cliff. It careened and began to skid.

Finally, Valerie removed her hands, but it was too late. Morley braked and downshifted, all the while fighting the oversized steering wheel. Then he screamed as the heavy bus splintered a guardrail and shot out into space. It landed for a moment on all four wheels, then rattled down the face of the cliff, until it flipped end-over-end and bounced, rolling over and over sideways, shedding glass and metal debris as it went. In a wake of flying sparks, it skidded upside down over snow-dusted boulders, then burst into flames, its metal skin ballooning from the blast.

* * *

Wallace Huff heard the explosions and called the police. Within the hour, he, Alex Zepeda, the bus dispatcher, and Isaac Whitson, the principal of Lincoln

Middle School, were at the site. In the numbing cold, they stood together off to one side, out of the way of police, firefighters, and paramedics who were busily working with an electric saw to cut away the hinges of the bus's emergency exit.

"Morley seemed normal enough this morning," said Zepeda.

"He must have had deep-rooted psychological problems, though," Whitson put in.

"Killed my boy," Wallace Huff said flatly. "Admitted it straight out."

Zepeda nodded sympathetically, then grimaced. "Eleven kids died because of him all those years ago. That's a lot of guilt to be carrying around. Guess it finally caught up with him."

Huff shook his head. "The way he was talking out front of my station, the man really thought that bus was full of the ghosts of those kids. He . . ." But a sudden silence stopped him.

Below, down at the burned-out hulk of the bus, the electric saw was turned off. Firefighters pulled on the emergency door. There was a metallic *crack* as the charred yellow section of metal gave way, then fell with a flop on the snow-covered hillside, sledding away on its own, down into the misty valley.

Paramedics and firefighters, flashlights in hand, quickly piled into the crumpled, smoke-blackened bus. Minutes later, they emerged dragging one body, Jack Morley's, which they zipped into a thick plastic bag and carried up the hill.

"Were there any others?" Whitson called to a grim-faced fire captain. "Were there any kids?"

"No," the man said, shaking his head.

"Well, that's it. The man's imagination went wild, totally insane," Whitson said to the others. "Thank goodness he read his route sheet wrong."

* * *

As an orderly in the Odessa County coroner's office, Quincy Anderson's take-home pay was a paltry $183 a week, hardly enough to live on. Now and then he'd find something of worth on the bodies as he prepared them for burial or autopsy. On the corpse of Jack Morley, there was nothing.

Curiously, however, clutched in Morley's left hand, Anderson found something that might be worth a few bucks. It was a small gold ring, a kid's ring, with the initials *V. S.* engraved inside.

Anderson pried it from Morley's fist. Then, looking around to make sure no one was watching, he stuffed it into his pocket, started whistling nonchalantly, then continued preparing the body for burial.

GROWING PAINS

It's getting worse every day. At my request, Mom and Dad have taken all the mirrors out of my room, but I can still see my hands and arms, and my body when I dress. Under my clothes I can feel it all over, and when I put my hands to my face I want to scream.

There is a knock at my door. "Ricky, are you in there?" asks my sister, Desiree.

I smile to myself, because it's such a stupid question. *Where else would I be? I've been in my bedroom for over a year now.*

"Can I come in?" she asks.

I wait for a second or two, thinking about it. "Sure, Des," I finally call back.

Desiree's sixteen now, two years older than I am, and three inches taller. I hate to admit it, but she is actually pretty good-looking, which seems impossible if you'd ever seen her as a little kid. She's trying to smile as she comes in, but she's not doing a very good job.

And she can't help it, but she's averting her gaze. She can't even look at me. It's too repulsive. *I'm* too repulsive.

"Got your lunch here," she says, stating the obvious, since she's carrying a tray with food on it.

"Thanks, Des," I say, looking at her ankles as I sit down in the chair at my desk.

I watch as Desiree puts the tray on my nightstand. There's spaghetti, salad, and a soda. I notice that the soda is root beer, which I really don't like that much. I could mention it, and Desiree, I know, would get me something else. But why bother? I'm not even really thirsty, or hungry, for that matter.

"Eat it before it gets cold," she says, smiling again, trying hard to act natural and cheerful.

"I will," I tell her.

"How're you feeling today?" she asks, edging toward the door.

"So-so."

"Mom says Dr. Colstein will be by later on."

"Yeah," I tell her. "I know."

"Mom says he wants to take more blood and tissue samples, and he's talking about a new treatment." Desiree shifts her weight uneasily from one foot to the other. "Maybe something will work this time, huh?"

I know I'm not making things very easy for her. In fact, I haven't been making things easy for anybody lately. Under the circumstances, it's hard for me to be nice. As the days pass and turn into an eternity, it's getting harder and harder for me to put on much of an act.

When I don't answer, Desiree starts moving toward

the door. "Well," she says, "let me, Dad, or Mom know if you want anything else."

"Okay, Des," I say, scratching at my face. I suddenly catch her staring at me.

She has horror in her eyes, and something else, too, guilt. I know how bad she feels about all this, and she's apologized a million times. But really, as I see it, she's no more to blame than anybody else. It's just something that happened. Maybe it was my dad's fault, my mom's, or, all things considered, mine.

"See ya," she says, shutting the door softly.

"Yeah," I say, alone again.

I push the TV remote control, then switch the channel to some weird sci-fi movie. It looks pretty cool, but it's hard for me to concentrate on it. My mind wanders and drifts back—as it has a thousand times before to when it happened, four years ago.

I was ten at the time. We had moved here to Pasadena, California, where my dad had started working at CTL, the Cellular Transmissions Laboratory. His project, his brainchild, was reintegrative molecular transport, RMT. Dad theorized that ordinary matter could be broken down into what he called its "particulate atomic structure," then electronically transported and reintegrated in its original form in a different place. What that means is that my dad was working on sending an object from one place to another by transmitting its molecules. For example, a ceramic plate could be sent, or beamed, from Los Angeles to Tokyo in a fraction of a second.

My dad started his work on RMT at the lab, but his regular duties took up too much of his time, so he moved his entire project to our basement. There he built two RMT modules, at opposite ends of the room. Each eight-by-fourteen-foot module, he hoped, would be able to both send and receive objects.

For two years he worked nights and weekends on his project. Some of his engineer friends, and sometimes even Mom, Desiree, and I, helped out.

But for the longest time he didn't have any success at all. In his first attempt at molecular transport, he tried to send a plastic cup from one module to another. Nothing happened. A few weeks later he tried again. This time, the only result was that the cup caught on fire and burned up. It was pretty frustrating for all of us.

It was almost a year before his first real breakthrough came, and it happened with a simple pair of scissors. One instant, they were in module *A*; the next, when he flipped a switch in the control box, the scissors were in module *B*.

"All right!" whooped Dad, looking more happy and excited than I'd ever seen him.

After that, it was pretty smooth sailing. Dad was sending all sorts of objects back and forth between the modules, pens, chairs, toys, lots of things. Now and then, there was a setback, though. Like when he transferred a book, Robert Louis Stevenson's *Treasure Island*. At first it looked like everything went fine. But then we noticed something kind of cool, but really strange. All the words were upside down and backward.

Then, a compact disc he sent came out with the music all scrambled, and a clock he transported started to run five minutes faster every hour. But we had faith in my dad, and it wasn't long before he had all the glitches worked out. Then he moved on to other things, like transporting live animals.

At first, my dad sent mice across the room. Then he tried guinea pigs. But just transporting things, even animals, across the basement, wasn't enough for my dad, I guess. So he went to Santa Fe, New Mexico, and set up a third module there. Then he started sending several items, and finally even a cat, from the module in Santa Fe right into module A in our basement in Pasadena.

Finally, my dad said the time had come for the final test. He flew to New Jersey where a fourth module had been set up to transport *him*.

When my dad got into the module in New Jersey, we were called in Pasadena to stand by. Then the controls were pushed and Dad was "molecularized." Can you believe that? My dad was reintegrated almost in the same instant from a module in New Jersey right into module A in our basement.

"Fantastic!" he exclaimed, beaming as he came out of the module.

"All right!" I cheered along with my mom and Desiree, and a room full of engineers, all clapping for my dad.

Actually, my mom didn't just cheer. She burst into tears, then ran over to my dad and gave him a great big hug and kiss. They were both so happy, smiling and jabbering out-of-control about becoming rich and famous. It was a pretty big day for all of us.

Until this point, the RMT project had been kept pretty hush-hush. Only a handful of people knew anything about it. Once my dad had this big success, meetings were held at CTL, and it was decided to "go public" with my dad's work. Larger and more sophisticated modules were designed for construction in Pasadena and even in London. Preparations were made for informing the media and explaining the process and uses of RMT. Finally, a huge public demonstration was planned. All of us, especially my dad, were very excited.

One Saturday morning, while Dad was at CTL working, Desiree and I were helping Mom outside in the yard and in the greenhouse, watering and planting flower seeds for asters, lobelias, and marigolds. Afterward, I was going to go over to the park and play basketball, but none of my friends were around when I called. Desiree didn't want to go, either. She was bored and grumpy.

"Well, let's do *something*," I said, starting to get into a bad mood myself.

Then all of a sudden her eyes lit up. "I know what we can do!" she said, all excited, and I knew exactly what she had in mind.

I followed her as she hurried down to the basement, and right off I started to get nervous. The two original RMT modules, like big, shiny glass eyes, were staring back at us.

"I'm going to transfer myself from *A* to *B*!" she exclaimed.

At first I was dead-set against it. "No way," I said, adamantly shaking my head. "It could be dangerous, and Dad would blow his top if he found out."

I just about had her talked out of it, but the more I argued why we shouldn't do it, the more I kept thinking about how great it would be. Eventually, I found I had talked Desiree out of it, but myself *into* it. In fact, I'd had a complete change of heart and was all set to go.

And so I did it. I climbed into module A and, one second later, after Desiree flipped the switch, I was in module B. To be honest, I was kind of disappointed. Yeah, the concept of moving from one place to another like that was fantastic, but when it came right down to it, I didn't really feel anything. It happened too fast, so fast that there really wasn't any sensation at all. It wasn't like going on a superfast roller coaster, or like being in a race car, or anything cool like that.

Desiree, though, was just about jumping out of her skin with excitement. "Wow! What was it like?" she asked the second I stepped out of module B.

"Nothing," I told her flatly.

I was about to go into more detail when we heard Mom calling us, so we shut off the RMT and headed upstairs.

*　*　*

It was a couple of days later, on a Tuesday morning, when the first sign started to happen. A pimple sprouted on my face right in the middle of my forehead. It was a weird one, kind of white and twisted looking, but hey, it was no big deal, it was a pimple. I shrugged it off and headed for school.

But by fourth period, during my history class, the pimple was bothering me a lot. In fact, my whole face felt funny, and I kept running my fingers over my skin and feeling lots of tiny bumps. Worst of all, some of the kids, especially Al Badenhauer, who sits next to me, were giving me weird looks.

"What?" I asked, shrugging. But everyone just looked away from me.

As soon as the bell rang, I hurried to the bathroom, and it was all I could do to keep from screaming when I saw my face. It was just awful. There were several big pimples, and the most horrible thing was that they weren't really pimples. They were little white things growing out of my pores.

"Gross, dude," said this guy named Ralph something-or-other.

"Hey, pizza face," said another jerk I didn't even know.

Even Brad Turner, a pretty good friend of mine, couldn't leave me alone. "What's wrong with your face, man?" he asked, not even bothering to hide his disgust. "That's a super weird case of acne you got there."

I didn't answer him. My complete attention was now focused on my arms and hands. They were starting to feel like my face, all tingly and hot, as if they were sprouting white squiggly things, too. I dropped my books right there in the bathroom and took off running, and I didn't stop until I reached my house.

When I walked in the door, I started screaming for someone right away, but no one was home. Frantic, I ran upstairs, tearing off my shirt as I went. Then I stopped dead in shock when I caught a glimpse of myself in the hall mirror. From my hands, arms, face, and chest, from almost everywhere, white, seedlike things were popping out from my pores. And, from some of them, I could see thin, white-green stems growing. At the end of a few of the stems, leaves were sprouting. They looked like the soft, wrinkly, spike-shaped leaves of asters.

Screaming hysterically, I ran to the kitchen and got the scissors. Then I started cutting the stems and leaves off my body, and digging out the seeds from my skin with my fingernails. My skin was practically bloody when I heard a car drive up.

A minute or two later Mom, Dad, and Desiree came in and found me in the kitchen. I was sitting on the tile floor in my underwear, with all this stuff that had come off me scattered all over the place. Horrified to have anyone see me like this, I ran upstairs and locked myself in the bathroom.

Within seconds, my dad was pounding on the door, begging for me to let him in. But I ignored him. I was sitting on the bathroom floor and crying, trying to concentrate as I held my dad's razor and shaving cream, prepared to shave off the stuff that was now sprouting again.

At first, the razor seemed like a great idea. It took most of the stuff off, except the stumps of stems and the seeds in my pores. But my back was a problem; I couldn't reach it. That's when I crawled to the door and unlocked it, letting my dad in. I definitely needed help.

"It's the seeds!" I screamed at my dad, who stood there looking at me in horror.

"What seeds?" he asked, confused and sickened. "What are you talking about? What's happening to you?"

"Dad," I said, sure I'd figured the whole terrible thing out. "I used the RMT, and I—"

"You what?!" he shouted.

"I'm sorry, Dad," I said, putting my hand up to stop him from going into a lecture. "Just listen. You see, right before I got into the module, I was planting flowers for Mom." I began to cry again. "Don't you see? There must have been some seeds on me, and they—"

"They integrated into your molecular makeup!" my dad finished my theory as he bent down to study the disgusting flesh on my arm.

It was about at that point that Mom and Desiree poked their heads into the bathroom and looked at me. "No!" I yelled, kicking the door closed. "Get away!"

I let only my dad stay. He took care of my back, then he shaved my head. It was so gross—the stems had started growing there, too. Then he rubbed me down with alcohol and witch hazel. That helped some. In fact, the seeds turned a funny brown color, and the stems hardly seemed to be growing at all. Then Dad decided to take me to the hospital.

The ambulance came in about three minutes flat and my dad rode with me in the back. He sat at my side, and kept saying encouraging things like, "Everything's going to be fine" and "We'll figure this all out," but neither he nor the paramedics had any idea what to do. There was revulsion and horror in their eyes, and even though they had rubber gloves on, I could tell they didn't want to touch me.

*   *   *

I spent over six weeks in the hospital, isolated in a room in the communicable disease section, even though it was determined pretty early on that what I had wasn't catching. A team of doctors examined me. Dermatologists, internists, geneticists, and hematologists poked and prodded me everywhere. Even a psychiatrist was called in, as if I had managed to create all this with my mind.

They tried everything, from freezing my skin, to rubdowns with all sorts of chemicals and medications, to small injections of what was essentially a poison. Everything worked a little for a while. Everything partly slowed the growth. But so far, nothing has completely stopped the growths from coming back again.

Finally, I was sent home. I went to my room, and in here I've been for more than a year. Twice daily, Dad gives me a complete rubdown with this funny-smelling mix of all sorts of things. I know he feels guilty, and I know how disappointed he is. After what happened to me, the RMT project was abandoned.

So, once a week, usually on Wednesdays, Dr. Colstein comes by. He gives me a checkup, and he usually tells me about some new "cure" he's working on. Maybe someday he'll actually find one. I hope so. I can't stand living like this much longer. I really can't.

I remember a long time ago, when I was about seven, my parents took Desiree and me to a car show. There was a woman there who had a terrible skin disease. It was so awful I couldn't even look at her. Just the quick glance I had of her gave me nightmares. Now I'm like her, only far, far worse.

Why do I say that my problem is worse? It's not just that a new flower is growing out of my body. (A marigold is growing out of my calf.) I can deal with that.

I'm not even surprised that something new is sprouting from me.

What bothers me is Desiree. I don't think she has noticed it yet, but when she came to bring my lunch, I saw an ugly, greenish bump on her ankle. It looked like an aster. She may have them all over her body soon. I'm sorry to say the doctors seem to be wrong about this thing being contagious. I wonder who will be next?

*P*hil was lying in the hospital bed, thinking about the accident. Dr. Huang Ti walked into the ward with a nurse, who slipped the gogglelike contraption over Phil's head. Phil blinked, and then . . .

* * *

He was sitting on a sparkling Caribbean beach with his mother, pulling on his diving suit.

"I'm not sure you ought to go scuba diving in these waters, Phil," his mom said anxiously. She looked out at the shimmering blue sea. "It's beautiful, but it also looks dangerous."

"Oh, come on, Mom," Phil said, rolling his eyes. "I'll be fine."

"But you heard what the man at the equipment rental shop said." She pointed out toward a ridge of dark rocks jutting above the surface. "He said those rocks are full of caves and moray eels. And if one of them sinks its teeth into you, you're likely to lose a leg or worse."

Phil sighed. "I'll stay away from the caves," he promised.

"Even so," his mom went on, "I just don't want you going out alone."

Phil groaned. "Mom, you paid for my scuba equipment and lessons back home. But now, when we're finally able to take this fantastic trip to the Caribbean, you don't want me to dive. And every day it's the same thing: 'Don't go out alone.' But who am I supposed to go out with? You can't swim, and I don't know anybody on the island."

"I see your point, honey, but . . ."

"Mom, I'll be okay," Phil said, flashing her a confident grin and kissing her on the cheek. "Don't worry, okay?"

A big sigh and a halfhearted smile meant his mom had finally given in. "All right," she said. "How much air do you have?"

"Two hours' worth, but I'll probably be back before then." And with that, Phil adjusted his air tank, flapped through ankle-deep water in his swim fins, bit into his mouthpiece, and gave a backward wave good-bye. He didn't want to see his mother's worried face.

Plowing through some gentle waves, Phil dived below the surface and was soon gliding in the silence and beauty of an all-water world. Being underwater was like watching a movie and being in it at the same time. The filtered sunlight shone like huge sheets of clear plastic, highlighting the bright colors of the fish that swam by him. Filled with a sense of wonder and challenge, Phil was having the time of his life.

Drifting along in awe, he was dreamily watching the underwater world go by, when suddenly a black wall loomed before him. Startled, it took him a moment to realize that it was one of the underwater ridges of rock the man at the equipment shop had warned him about. He had promised his mom he'd keep away from them, too.

Briefly, he thought about resurfacing. But something, perhaps his fascination with being so near danger, kept him from going up. Instead, he went deeper, and before he knew it, Phil found himself swimming close to a large gap in the rock. His heart pounding, he entered the gap. It turned out to be a dark tunnel.

I'll just take a quick look, he told himself. But the tunnel was so awesome, he couldn't stop. He just kept going deeper and deeper down the corkscrewing crevice.

Slowly, a feeling of unease crept over him, yet there was no sign of danger. *Enough's enough!* he warned himself. *I'm getting out of here.* In the cramped space, he turned to head back out. Suddenly a giant eel floated out of a hole, its eyes glaring at him, its ugly mouth opening and closing.

Terrified, Phil backed deeper into the tunnel, away from the twisting black-brown creature. His eyes wide, he watched as it rolled inward and backward, and then disappeared into the rocks.

That was close! Phil's mind raced. His heart pounded like a jackhammer and he began to inch forward when another moray appeared from below. In one quick flash a viselike pain shot through his foot, as the eel's jaws sliced right through his fin. He kicked like crazy until his fin flew off and he screamed at the monster so violently he almost lost his mouthpiece. Then he swam as if his life depended on it, heading deeper and deeper into the murky tunnel.

Suddenly he was on the surface again, but he could hardly see. It was as though he'd come up and found that night had fallen. For a moment he thought his fear had driven him crazy, and then he realized he was in an underwater cavern, a dark, slimy room made of rock with a jagged ceiling and a floor filled with stale-smelling black seawater.

His fingers scraping a trail in the slime, he hoisted himself up onto a rock. Then he turned off his air-flow valve and took off his mask.

At first he was grateful for the apparent safety the place offered. But very quickly a new fear settled over him. The cave was actually a death trap, a black coffin of slowly rising water. There was only one escape from the incoming tide, and that was back through the tunnel of huge slithering eels.

Numb with terror, Phil clung to the slick rock and cried out. Again and again he shouted for help, but his voice just echoed emptily inside the cave. And then he almost had to laugh at himself. Who could hear him? Who could help him? Who could rescue him from an underwater coffin?

Already the water was lapping around the rock where Phil was sitting. As he hoisted himself higher, he glimpsed a flash of movement as a spider crab scrambled across the back of his hand. Jumping with fright, he lost his balance, and before he knew what was happening, he skidded down the slippery rock. With a loud splash, he belly-flopped into the dark pool.

A few quick strokes and Phil was back out of the water. The salt stung his eyes, but he had seen something while he was scrambling out of the water. On the opposite wall of the cave was a dim shaft of light. Now, as he looked harder, he could see that it was lighter where the ceiling slanted down on that side.

Could it be an air hole? he wondered. *Of course it was!* He should have known there'd be one. Perhaps it was a way out. Hope rising within him for the first time, he reasoned that when the water rose high enough, he could swim to the air hole, try to squeeze through, and head for the surface.

He looked at the rapidly rising water. The tide was almost full. In some spots, the water was actually touching the low-hanging ceiling, and already it was up to his chest. Time, Phil knew, was quickly running out. He would have to act soon . . . or not act at all.

Carefully he checked his air valve, then pulled down his face mask. *Don't think about the eels,* he told himself. *Don't think about anything but reaching the surface.*

But the eels were all Phil could think about. He knew that if they were in the cave, they would probably attack him. But he also knew something else: this was the only chance he would have to save himself. And so, biting down on his mouthpiece and turning on the air flow from his tank, he slipped into the water.

Because the water was so murky, Phil had to come

up twice to relocate the hole, and on the second attempt, he smacked his head against a low-hanging rock. "Argh!" he screamed, biting his mouthpiece. His forehead throbbed with pain. But that didn't matter. *Nothing* mattered except reaching the opening, and surviving.

He quickly ducked under the water for a third try, and this time Phil found the gap. Reaching through and grabbing a rocky handhold, he pulled himself up. Then he twisted and turned, desperately trying to squeeze through the opening.

But it was hopeless. The hole was just too small.

Phil wasn't surprised. He had never really expected to get through. All along, deep down, he had known that the only way out was back through the tunnel opening, back through the eels.

Resolved to the horrible task ahead, he pushed himself free, and plunged deep into the water, searching for the tunnel opening at the bottom of the cave's interior. But where was it? Where had he entered into this black coffin?

With his air dwindling by the minute, Phil desperately searched for the tunnel entrance, but it just wasn't there. Nearly insane with fear, he struck out in the opposite direction. But again, he found no entrance. Baffled, breathing in more and more of his precious air supply, Phil literally started to swim around in circles until suddenly, he felt something pulling at his legs. It was the tide. The sheer force of it was sucking him backward.

"No!" he screamed into his mouthpiece, fighting with everything he had. But he had no control. His hands and shoulders, and then his air tank, scraped against rock walls as he rolled and twisted in the powerful current.

Phil was so disoriented that he didn't know which way to go. All he knew was that he had to keep moving. He was sure the eels were everywhere, coiled in the rocks, watching him, ready to attack at any moment.

And then Phil spotted what he feared the most. Right in front of him were the two dead-looking eyes of an eel, gazing out from a crevice in the coral. Nearly gagging with fear, he watched in horror as it uncoiled from its hiding place, unfurling its ugly, black-brown body in a hideous loop. Then, with its mouth opened wide, exposing rows of tiny, needlelike teeth, the eel struck, clamping its jaws *not* on him, but on a gray fish swimming nearby that Phil had not even seen.

And then everything went black.

*   *   *

Carol Lawton, Phil's mother, made her way into the neurosurgical wing of Northside Community Hospital in Dayton, Ohio. Dr. Huang Ti looked up at her approach and greeted her warmly.

"Phil is doing well, today, Ms. Lawton," said the doctor.

"But, doctor, I'm worried."

"Worried about what, Ms. Lawton?"

"I still keep asking myself if what we're doing is right."

The doctor paused thoughtfully before answering. "Ms. Lawton, four years ago, after Phil's neck was broken in that fall from a tree, he was paralyzed from the neck down. He wanted to die. He had nothing to live for, no hope of ever leading an active, happy life.

"But look at him now!" The doctor's eyes brightened. "Through VRQ, Virtual Reality for Quadriplegics, your son is thriving, *living* again." Dr. Huang Ti gestured toward a windowed ward in which Phil and several other young people lay paralyzed in their beds. Each patient had gogglelike contraptions over their faces.

"He does look totally absorbed," Carol Lawton admitted.

"Today," said the doctor, "Phil believes he is in the Caribbean with you, and he is having the adventure of his life, fighting his way out of an underwater cave."

* * *

Phil watched as the eel sank its teeth into the hapless fish. Then the eel recoiled, and retreated to feast on its prize in the privacy of some dark, rocky chamber.

Taking advantage of the eel's distraction, Phil struck out with new vigor, his arms and legs moving powerfully as he swam swiftly down the tunnel. Then, all at once, the walls opened up, and he was out of the black cave and back in bright water.

He could still see the eels and feel their rubbery coils against his legs, but they were only a horrible memory now. Still, as if he were being pursued, Phil swam hard, until finally he broke the surface. After the gloom of the cave, the sunlight nearly blinded him. He spat out his mouthpiece and gulped in the fresh air. Then he jumped as something rubbery brushed against him.

Whipping around, Phil burst out laughing. It was just a harmless inflatable life preserver.

"There, now, young man," someone called from a boat. "Didn't mean to scare you. You just take hold of that ring and rest yourself. We'll have you into the boat in no time." He waved to someone in another boat. "Over here!" he yelled. "We've found him, ma'am!"

Phil could see only shadows in the glare of the sun, but he recognized one shadow. It was his mother! She was leaning over the side of the little boat, her arms stretched out to him, while tears of joy streamed down her face.

HORROR, ROUND-TRIP

"**Y**ou're going to be fine, Carlie," said my dad.

"You're going to have a great time. Dallas is a fun city," said my mom.

"Yeah, sure," I said, trying to plaster a smile on my face, knowing they were just saying the kinds of things parents are supposed to say when their only child is going away solo for the first time. "I'll be fine," I said, putting up a fairly convincing brave front to reassure them. I knew, however, that deep down they were probably as apprehensive about the trip as I was.

The next morning I was going to fly to Dallas to visit my grandparents. I felt nervous. Forget butterflies, I felt like I had snakes. Even though I wanted to spend the summer with my grandparents, I had an ominous feeling about being away from home for so long. I was also feeling weird about flying. I'd never even been on an airplane before, and now here I was flying for the first time alone.

117

I went to bed around 11:00 P.M. But I couldn't sleep. After my parents gave me long, drawn-out goodnight speeches and hugs, I kept worrying about the trip. All sorts of dark, sick thoughts crept into my head, like getting sucked out of a window and falling forever through space. Or I imagined the walls of the plane slowly collapsing inward and crushing everybody inside. I tossed and turned, my body so tense it ached, my neck muscles all tied up in knots.

Beside my bed, the clock ticked past 2:00 A.M. I was really getting stressed out, so I got up, splashed water on my face, and walked around in our dark, quiet condo trying to relax. It was almost 3:00 A.M. before I crawled back into bed. Still, I just lay there, my mind going around in an endless circle of unwanted thoughts. Soon I gave up trying to get any sleep at all. It was clear I was just going to lie there like that all night.

But somewhere along the line I must have fallen asleep, because suddenly it was morning, and my dad was touching me on the shoulder, telling me to get up. My mom was also trying to wake me, calling me from the next room to come downstairs for breakfast. Feeling strange and half-asleep, I forced myself out of bed, dressed, and went down to the kitchen.

Later, while my mother double-checked my suitcase, my father gave me a lot of advice about where to sit on the plane. I guess he forgot that I was almost thirteen, because he also told me what to say to the flight attendant, and how to call him collect if there was a problem. I think he felt bad that he had to work and couldn't drive out to the airport with my mother and me, so I listened to him to make him feel better. Actually, I was just too exhausted to really care about whether he was coming to the airport, or that he was treating me like a baby.

Before I knew it, my mom and I were on the freeway and already approaching the exit for the airport. Deep inside, I wanted to stay in the car forever, because as long as I was driving with my mother, I felt safe, sure that none of the horrors I'd thought of the night before could happen.

But the drive seemed to go by in a blur, almost as if we were in a fast-forward movie, and we reached the terminal in no time at all. More nervous than ever, I felt as if I weren't just going away, but that I was going away forever, and never coming back. I wanted to scream at my mother, "No, I can't go!" But I knew that was ridiculous. I had to see this thing through. I owed it to my parents, who were looking forward to some time alone, to my grandparents who were expecting me, and to myself, so I could conquer this absurd fear.

My mom obviously realized how I felt, because three times she repeated the whole now-there's-nothing-to-worry-about routine. And with each repetition she went over all the reasons why I was going to have a fantastic time. "Still, Carlie, I'm going to miss you—a *little,*" she said teasingly, a smile on her face but sadness in her eyes.

I nodded and told her the summer would be over before she knew it. I guess I was saying that for the both of us. Then I promised to write often, and we hugged and said our good-byes. It all seemed to go that fast, the drive to the airport, our talk, checking in my baggage.

Within minutes I was on board the plane.

As soon as I stepped into the cabin, the butterflies, snakes, worms, or whatever seemed to inhabit my nervous stomach, started swirling around again. Then, before I knew it, we taxied out onto the runway, the jet engines screamed, and the plane went shrieking upward into the air.

I felt so lonely I could hardly stand it. *This is silly,* I scolded myself. *How can you feel lonely surrounded by all these other passengers?*

I looked around the packed plane and wondered where exactly all these people were going when we landed. I wondered why they had chosen this particular flight, and what their plans were. All of them seemed unusually quiet and sad looking.

To my right, there was a man with two little blond-haired boys, twins, about four years old, dressed up in matching navy blue blazers. They were squirming around in their seats, playing with toy airplanes, and constantly dropping them on the floor. From my aisle seat, I tried to catch their father's eye. He seemed to be traveling alone with the boys, and since I've done a lot of baby-sitting, I thought I'd offer to give him a hand with his kids on the flight. I figured it would give me something to do and keep my mind off my fears.

With all the commotion his kids were causing, it took awhile, but the man finally caught my eye and looked straight at me. I smiled and was just about to make my offer, when I noticed that he wasn't smiling back. In fact, he just stared at me for a minute and turned away. *Well, so much for trying to be friendly,* I thought, leaning back in my seat.

The whole thing made me feel worse than ever. I just knew something horrible was going to happen. I didn't know what, but I knew it was going to be really bad.

You've got to stop this, I told myself. *Everything is going to be all right.* I settled back in my seat, feeling ill from nervousness and lack of sleep. Then, taking a deep breath, I closed my eyes and forced myself to relax. Soon, the steady drone of the plane became comforting, almost pleasant, and I felt myself dozing off.

* * *

When I awoke, I had no idea how much time had passed. All I knew was that suddenly I was wide awake, and instantly aware that something was wrong . . . *very* wrong. My eyes bounced back and forth, looking from one end of the plane to the other, and what I saw just didn't make any sense. The plane was empty!

What's going on? my mind raced, thinking back to when I boarded the plane, to when we took off. Every seat had been filled. I was sure of it, but now there was no one in the whole cabin except me.

My head throbbed. It felt like it was expanding and about to explode. *Are you going insane?* I kept asking myself. *Are you crazy? Are you? Are you?*

"Hello?" I called down the empty aisle. "Is anyone else on this plane?"

Looking for someone, *anyone,* I ran down the aisle. Then I screamed for help, but no one was there to hear me. In fact, except for the whine of the jets, there was no sound at all.

Terrified, I edged past some seats and looked out a

window. Thousands of feet below was a sprawling city, full of people that I couldn't see, and who couldn't see or hear me. *Did they know I was up here?* I thought wildly. *Did my parents know where I was?*

I gasped, trying to force air into my panicked lungs, but I could barely breathe. "Calm down!" I yelled at myself. "Try to think! The plane is still in the air, so *someone* must be flying it."

I ran forward and opened the cockpit door, then gaped in horror. The cockpit was empty, too! The plane, it seemed, was flying by itself.

Now my whole body was shaking, and the hair on the back of my neck was standing straight up. "Am I losing my mind?" I called out to no one. "Is that what's happening? Please!" I begged. "If anyone is here, tell me what's going on!"

In a blind panic, I shut the door to the cockpit and began to run toward the rear of the aircraft, convinced that I had to get away from whoever, or whatever, was flying it. For now I was sure that some unearthly force had taken control of me and the plane. Yes, that was it. Some alien being was going to appear soon, and I had to find a place to hide. In terror I ran down the aisle, my heart beating like a jackhammer.

But I seemed to be running in slow motion, and the cabin was growing colder and darker by the minute. Suddenly there was silence. I froze and listened, and, to my horror, I realized that the engines had stopped.

Instantly, the plane tilted downward, then began to lose altitude. I lurched down the aisle, desperately grabbing at the armrests, the chair backs, anything to stop my fall. The lights, already flickering, suddenly went out, plunging the plane into complete darkness. Filled with my screams, the plane turned into a metal coffin, hurtling toward earth.

I curled up in a ball, waiting for the impact that would end my life. Then I heard a voice. Someone was calling my name through the darkness! I was trying to get up, but I couldn't. Again, I heard the voice, much nearer now and louder. Then, someone, or something, touched me.

I opened my eyes. My father was bending over me, shaking me by the shoulder. "Are you all right, Carlie?" he asked. "It's time to get up."

I blinked, staring at him as he walked out of the room. My dream, my nightmare, had been so real I was having trouble believing that I was in my own room, in my own bed, and that the whole ugly thing had just been a bad dream. I felt confused, caught somewhere between the terror of my nightmare and the relief of being at home and smelling breakfast cooking. In a daze, I got out of bed and put on my clothes, as flashes of the dream came back to me.

Then a weird feeling, a sense of dread, and of something else, came over me. It seemed as if everything I was doing I'd done before, as if each move I was making was a reenactment of an earlier move. Step by step, I felt as if I was reliving the whole nightmare. Only now I was awake. Or was I?

When my mom and I got to the airport, the same thought kept going through my mind. And later, as I sat on the plane, waiting for it to take off, I kept wondering if I had really just had a weird dream or had somehow received a warning of what was to come. I closed my eyes and tried to relax, and felt myself dozing off.

Suddenly, someone touched me on the shoulder, and I jumped.

"I didn't mean to scare you," said a man, "but I saw you saying good-bye to your mother. I hope you don't mind if my boys and I sit with you. I could really use help with them on the flight."

Peeking from behind their father were two little blond-haired boys, twins, about four years old, all dressed up in matching navy blue blazers.

If you liked *The Trap Door*, you'll love . . .

THE FRIGHT MASK
& Other Stories to Twist Your Mind

When it comes to terror, there's a lot more in store in *The Fright Mask*, the second volume of *Screamers*. You'll find nine new nightmares that will startle and delight you, especially once you discover the surprise ending in each twisted tale.

For example, in "Snapshots of the Dead," no one believes Tanya Field's claim that she traveled back in time to ancient Egypt . . . until an archeologist digs up a mysterious 5,000-year-old mummy and learns the terrible truth. Like the hero of the scary story, "Sabrina," you'll never guess just who's pulling the strings in this bizarre story about a wisecracking puppet who seems to have a life of its own.

For a sneak preview, just turn the page. It's a real scream!

0-8167-3722-3 • $3.50 / $4.75 Can.

Available wherever you buy books.

THE FRIGHT MASK
& Other Stories to Twist Your Mind

Billy looked in his Halloween treat bag. There were only a few things in it. It would be embarrassing to go home with so little to show for the evening. His mom and dad would be disappointed that he wasn't fitting in . . . again. The almost-empty bag would be proof that he'd been a flop, that he hadn't found a group to hook up with.

It had not been easy, being the new kid in town. He had no friends and all the kids he'd asked to go trick-or-treating with had just laughed at him. He didn't even have a costume, so maybe it was better to be alone, Billy thought.

Across the vacant lot, headed straight at him through the dark, came a rowdy group of trick-or-treaters, laughing wildly.

"I'm going to suck his blood," said a make-believe Dracula, plastic fangs clicking in his mouth as he walked up with the others.

A girl with her face powdered to a ghastly white and with huge black circles drawn around her eyes giggled. "I'm Dracula's wife," she said. "Who are you supposed to be?" she asked Billy. "A nerd?"

"A nerd, it is," said a pirate with a black patch over his eye and a fake hook for a hand, and a cardboard sword in his belt. "Let's see what plunder he has in his bag, maties," he snarled, grabbing at Billy's treat bag.

"Leave me alone!" snapped Billy, pulling his bag away just in the nick of time.

"Better give Long John Silver what he wants," a boy with a fake knife stuck in his head and fake blood all over his face growled. "Better give it to him, or you'll end up like me, with a pain in the brain."

The group thought this was the funniest thing they'd ever heard, and they were all now in a circle around Billy, laughing and joking. The pirate began poking him with his cardboard sword, and Dracula snarled at him with fake fangs. Billy's palms began to sweat, and he had a sinking feeling inside. He recognized these kids. They were all the kids he'd asked to go trick-or-treating earlier that day.

"How come you're by yourself, twerp?" Brad Kelly asked, laughing. "Too cheap to buy a mask?" Brad added with a sneer. "Or too stupid?"

"Maybe his mommy couldn't think of a costume for her nerdy son," Josh Steinberg cracked as he adjusted the knife in his head, "so he went as a geek."

"My mom made a great costume," Billy practically roared. "You're just too blind to see it.

"Uh-oh," said Brad sarcastically. "Little Billy's getting mad."

"My mother made me a costume *and* a mask," Billy repeated. "I'm wearing the mask right now. It's the mask of a normal boy."

Pete just laughed at him. "You aren't normal, dude. You're—"

But suddenly the air went out of his voice. Then his snide expression disappeared and turned to one of complete terror. Suddenly, the teasing stopped. All Billy could hear now, he thought happily, were the terrified screams of his cruel classmates. It would be a Halloween they'd never forget.